DIAMONDS THROUGH WATERLOO

DIAMONDS THROUGH WATERLOO

BOOK I:
T-REPORTS

Larry Forcey

Diamonds through Waterloo: T-Reports

To Brandon, Ryan, Mara, and Abby—

Remember.

Acknowledgments

Thank you, Karen Cleghorn, for proofing, editing, and suggesting. You made the story tighter and helped it move with less disruption. I would also like to express my appreciation to *Inksnatcher* for their assistance with cover design.

Most of the baseball books I have read include appreciation for individuals who assisted with research, particularly employees at the Hall of Fame in Cooperstown, New York. The research, however, for this manuscript was conducted in the solitary confines of an office, behind a computer.

Details of the historical events described in the narrative would not have been possible without the access provided to Daily Editions available through Newspapers.com. I often found myself transported to another era as I read articles written over one hundred years earlier.

The ease of accessing this information is testament of the great blessing of living in the digital age and the hard work of those over the past century who helped preserve the legacy of print.

Where is the genius who can explain the wonderful hold baseball has on the American public? It was no inhumane desire to see a bull fight or a bloody contest that drew the immense throng to the American league park yesterday, but a wholesome boyish desire to see the greatest ball teams on earth come together and battle for supremacy . . .

—Boston Globe, October 4, 1903

Prologue

BEGINNING OF THE BIG INNING

Wtilliam John Jennings was born between Sunday and Tuesday.

The medical staff concluded he was delivered between the late evening hours of June 6 and the dawn of the 8th. Unable to determine anything further, they marked the case as priority for the Board of Special Inquiry.

A crew member discovered the child during a routine late evening inspection of the decks on Wednesday, June 9. The lights around the ship's perimeter were low, and although the moon was bright, it was just past its first quarter, slightly above the horizon, providing little illumination. Descending the stairwell from the *Noordland*'s first-class cabins, the watchman paused. Most evenings the deck was scattered with second-class passengers seeking fresh ocean air, but this night he saw no one along the entire portside until he passed under a lifeboat.

He stopped when he saw her.

Several yards ahead nestled between two white pillars, a woman stood, leaning forward on the outside of the ship's protective railings, her arms reaching behind and grasping the metal rails. Before he had a chance to speak, she released her hands and disappeared.

He raced to where she had stood, swinging his arms, reaching for a leg or a piece of clothing. But by the time he arrived at the edge, it was hopeless. Below him was a blanket of dark, impossible to see any sign of her attempt to stay afloat, no splashing, no lingering concentric rings of water that marked her departure. Just black.

Hanging his head, he noticed a shallow pool of liquid on the deck where the woman had stood. He lowered himself to his knees and extended his hand, recoiling at the warm, thick, slippery texture. He followed the trail of blood to his left, toward the stairwell, and down to the lower level of the ship. The trail continued past the steerage cabins to the stalls for livestock and on to the infant.

***

The *Noordland* arrived in New York Harbor on Thursday, June 10, in the late afternoon. Just minutes earlier, the chief immigration officer, Alexander Chalmers, had left his office and boarded the ferry for Battery Park, returning to his young family on the Lower East Side.

Alexander approached work each morning with trepidation and left each evening with reluctance. Despite the daily certainty of difficult decisions and the family he longed to return to, by the time he had entered his rhythm of work and immersed himself in the cases of those he served, it was difficult to leave the paperwork on his desk. Sheets filled with unfinished business held the fates of individuals, their futures dependent upon his wisdom, diligence, and mercy.

In the mornings he awoke with this mixture of fear and excitement—a feeling of inadequacy along with the honor of service. He savored those first moments of the day, the quiet assurance that he had awakened earlier than most of his neighbors. As his eyes adjusted to the darkness around him, he anticipated the rituals of the morning: savoring the aroma of coffee while watching the figure of his wife, Sarah, silhouetted by the large candle on the dining table, the flame illuminating her slight features onto the curtains separating their bedroom from the kitchen. Somehow, his sense of value rose as he reached for his uniform, buttoned the olive-green short-sleeved shirt to the top, wrapped the black tie around the collar, and pushed it snugly into place. The morning routine was complete as he approached Sarah, embraced her from behind, kissed the top of her head, walked quietly to his children's bedsides, and bent to kiss his daughter and son atop their heads while they slept.

On most days he was the first to leave the six-story structure in which thirty-five other families resided. The neighborhood was growing at an alarming rate. Some of the apartments had over ten occupants. He and his wife and two children were one of the fortunate families that did not feel their home bursting.

As he looked north toward Houston Street, then south toward Grand, Hester, and Canal, he saw sides of buildings draped with carpets, bedsheets, and mattresses, evidence of the need for an apartment's occupants to relieve their home of articles saturated with the smells of overcrowding. The dense population from several blocks south had not yet reached them, but the effects were stretching to all the neighboring streets of Manhattan's lower east end.

Many of Alexander's friends suggested he ought to lobby management to find ways of slowing the influx of newcomers from across the Atlantic. He understood their concern and was worried himself, for his children in particular, of the increasing ease with which disease spread in the densely populated conditions. Yet in the midst of it all, he celebrated the new arrivals, recognizing their existence as providing the income required to sustain his family. And there was a more surreptitious reason for celebrating whenever he saw another ship on the horizon making its way into the East River. For each new arrival could be carrying in their parcels or their memory the ingredients for some new culinary creation that had yet to emerge into the neighboring streets. The Polish had concentrated on the western end of Canal Street, and he often walked out of his way to or from the elevated train when he felt the desire to tease his senses with the simmering, savory scents of sausages. Somewhere on Canal—he was not quite sure where—the number of Polish neighbors lessened and the concentration of Russians increased, lending to a whole new array of stimuli.

The filth in the alleys, the horse waste on the streets, and the millions of people living within a few square miles of one another created a pungent odor. Despite this, during a string of humid summer days, a strong breeze from the East River carried the aroma of the culinary creations of his neighbors—sausages, borsch, goulash, Kiev. Each was a spark, a potent reminder that joy and beauty could be found in these streets where there was putrid odor, disease, and death.

None of the scents, however, enticed him more than the one he experienced in the early morning hours on his walk to the elevated train that transported him to Battery Park. He closed his eyes when he first stepped from his home, stopped just outside the door, raised his head toward heaven, and breathed deeply. He enveloped within his breast as much as he could of the sweet aroma released from hundreds of ovens, forming what he imagined as a cloud of manna, and butter, and sugar, and comfort. His path led him to Rafael's on the corner of Broadway and Rivington, where he purchased a newspaper and a Danish. He ascended the stairs and awaited the train's arrival.

He would not open the paper until he boarded the train and found a seat. The wait on the platform was reserved for the enjoyment of his pastry. Reading the paper would require a reach inside his jacket and the effort to situate his glasses onto his nose.

He glanced at the headlines long enough to read the bold print just as he heard the train approaching. There was a story of President McKinley holding a rally in Kentucky, another of continued public outcry against Tammany. There was a cable car accident, a trolley accident, a tornado that killed six in his home state of Iowa.

The train stopped and its doors opened. Alexander entered, sat, sighed, and smiled, grateful for finding an open seat so easily, but feeling a tinge of guilt for having no desire to read or learn more of the suffering alluded to in the headlines. Instead, he reached into his jacket, put on his glasses, and turned to page three—the sports stories of the day.

His Brooklyn Bridegrooms had beaten Pittsburgh but still were in fifth place, far behind the league-leading Orioles. The season was young, but Baltimore was showing no signs of weakening. They had won the first three Temple Cups, and they were showing signs of dominating for a fourth consecutive year. They had played thirty-six games and lost only nine. Although the Bridegrooms also had a winning record, they had lost twice as many games. Worse, attending their games did not guarantee much excitement. Often they were low-scoring affairs, and though the players were competent, they did not play with the same flamboyance as the team from Baltimore.

Perhaps it was not a fair comparison, but it was unavoidable. After attending an Orioles game with his friend Thomas Kemp, he was hooked. The team had revolutionized the sport with their double steals, hard-grinding determination, and chops. They had discovered that by deliberately hitting down on the ball with as much force as possible, it resulted in the batter safely reaching base with as much frequency as hitting a clean live drive. Watching one of their games was like watching a circus of ballplayers doing things the fans did not dream possible. They raced around the bases while their opponents scrambled to find ways to defend against their antics.

It was not the Orioles team for which Alexander cheered, but for the players themselves. He was certain that other fans felt as he did—fond of the O's skills, hoping their own home team would soon adopt Baltimore's style of play. Alexander studied the results of the last home game, as he thought they were out of character. Baltimore had only beaten the Cleveland Spiders by the score of 4–2. The previous day was more akin to the norm—they had outscored Cleveland 11–6. A few days earlier they had scored ten runs against Cincinnati. In mid-May they had scored twenty runs in one game against St. Louis, and during that same trip they scored a total of forty-five runs in just three games.

Reading the scores was a daily diversion that seemed to always usher his arrival at Battery Park with increased rapidity. The ferry would not leave until he boarded, so he made a habit of allowing other passengers to exit the train before he disembarked. Once it had emptied, he stood, rolled the paper and placed it under his arm, walked through the park to the dock, and boarded the ferry.

The weather felt arid, more like an early fall morning than a humid mid-June day. To his left was the gateway for ships traveling from Europe. He ventured daily onto the perimeter of the island to view one or more ships as they arrived, smiling as passengers pressed against one another to catch their first sight of Lady Liberty or the skyline of the city.

Alexander enjoyed the satisfaction of resolving complications many immigrants brought with them, issues that had to be settled before they were allowed to leave the island and enter their new lives. But it was the solving of problems he enjoyed, the resolution, the end of the ordeal. He never looked forward to the presentation of a new task that awaited him. His best days were when he arrived at the island's dock, left the ferry, and walked to his office without being intercepted by a coworker awaiting his arrival, ready to explain the complexities of a new case.

Immediately, he sensed something was not right. As the ship's crew maneuvered to dock, he saw the chief surgeon, Dr. Joseph White, standing at the point where immigration employees turn right and medical staff turn left. The doctor was somber, arms crossed, head bobbing.

Alexander was the last to leave, allowing coworkers to exit before he stepped ashore. As he neared the end of the dock, his eyes met the doctor's. The doctor nodded, stepped back, jerked his head toward the left, and began walking.

Though Dr. White was a military man and ran the island's hospital with order and efficiency, there was an atmosphere of comradery and lightness among his staff. Alexander often visited the doctor's home that was built at the tip of the south side of the island, several hundred yards from the hospital. He found it to be an oasis on an island of turmoil. Three large oaks stood in the front, shading the two-story house, and a white fence separated the home's porch from the front yard. Five upstairs windows looked down upon the island, and two large windows stood on each side of the front door.

Most of his encounters with the doctor were necessitated by work, but often, when a day was not filled with urgency, he ventured here, hoping the doctor was free for lunch or a walk. They would talk of current affairs or baseball or their families. Alexander's daughter, Ruth, was four, and his son, Elimelech, was two. He could seek advice as they grew and entered new stages, hoping the doctor's rearing of four children may bring insight.

The doctor had not yet spoken as they walked from the ferry, his brisk pace more determined than usual and his path leading them not toward the buildings of the infirmary but toward his home.

When they reached the front door, the doctor stopped and held out his arm. "Alexander, extra care is needed with this one."

Alexander entered the home and noticed a mug of coffee on the dining table, still hot enough to billow streams of heat, and a stack of papers set to its right. Not needing further instruction, he sat, reached for his glasses in his coat pocket, looped the wire-like frames over his ears, and picked up the papers.

The first few pages were the manifests from the *Noordland*, a ship that had arrived the previous day. Manifests were normally several pages in length, a dozen pages or so, depending upon the size of the ship, but this stack of pages was in the hundreds. He thumbed past the manifest and noticed detailed interviews, apparently of the people listed on the manifest, organized based upon whether they were crew or a passenger in first class, second class, or steerage.

He looked up at the doctor.

"These are all crew? And passengers?"

"Yes," Dr. White answered.

"But, why? Am I to read them all?"

The doctor sat, shaking his head, pulling up a chair to the right of Alexander. "No," he answered. "The interviews were necessary to confirm our fears."

Alexander studied his friend, curious, but confident he would explain.

"A child was found on board. No parents."

The doctor scratched his beard and fidgeted in his chair. He pulled it closer to the table. "Alexander, he's an infant, born on board. Just a few days old. We've no idea who the parents might be."

Alexander nodded slowly and somberly, gazing at the stack of pages, with a growing sense of inadequacy. He had that same awful feeling he had when presented with a new case—that perception of having no recourse or resource with which to formulate a plan of action—a feeling of being totally unmatched for the task. He wasn't even sure what to ask. There were so many questions and scenarios darting through his mind, none of which would help him solve anything but would muddy the path to resolution. He closed his eyes and took a deep sigh.

"We know the mother is not one of the passengers?" he asked, fairly certain of the doctor's response.

"That is correct," Dr. White confirmed. "The crew recognized immediately the unique nature of the situation and discreetly conducted interviews of all first- and second-class passengers prior to entering the harbor."

Alexander nodded.

Dr. White continued. "The ship's medical personnel were aware of no passengers who were close to delivery. I met with them last night and am confident that their reports are accurate—the mother was not among the *Noordland*'s first- or second-class passengers."

"And steerage?"

The doctor shook his head. "We examined them all last night, into the early morning hours of today. Nothing. Four expectant mothers boarded in Antwerp. All four are still expecting."

Placing his hands on each side of his head, Alexander slumped over the stack of papers. "And your worst fear?" he muttered.

"The night watchman witnessed a woman on Wednesday evening leap from the second deck. A trail of blood led him to the child."

"And the board?" Alexander asked. "They are aware?"

Dr. White shook his head. "None were here when the ship arrived. They were all with you on the ferry last night. It will be on the docket this morning. Perhaps this afternoon you should be prepared to discuss options."

Alexander reached for the mug he had not yet raised to his lips. He slowly poured the lukewarm coffee into his mouth, consuming it with five swallows. He placed the mug back onto the table, stood, and scooped the stack of papers into his arms, holding them out before him as though he were carrying them to an altar.

THE BIG INNING

For the next three hours he immersed himself in the *Noordland*'s records,

manifest, crew testimonies, and the account of the night watchman. Two hundred seventy-three passengers were recorded on the ship's manifest when it departed Antwerp on Sunday, May 30, and two hundred seventy-three were on the Recapitulation Ledger when the ship arrived in New York Harbor on Wednesday, June 9. Some ships had reputations for providing safe passage regularly for stowaways, but the *Noordland* was not one of them. It had already made the passage from Antwerp to New York four times since January, and there had been no recorded stowaways. And technically, this was still true, if in fact the woman who gave birth to the child and abandoned ship had boarded the *Noordland* illegally prior to the departure.

The *Noordland*'s chief physician signed the Affidavit of Surgeon, certifying that he had examined all first- and second-class passengers, and hand wrote an addendum confirming that there were no women who showed signs of recently giving birth. Next to the surgeon's affidavit was the certification of the commanding officer, confirming the recapitulation count of passengers and verifying that there were no loathsome or dangerous felons among those listed on the *Noordland*'s manifest.

As Alexander studied the documents further, he grouped the passengers into nationalities, hoping desperately to find any clue that may help identify whether the child had some relation to one of those on board. There were twenty-four Americans returning from vacation, eighty-three Austrians, fifty Germans, twenty-five Russians, twenty-one Hungarians, fifteen Belgians, and smaller numbers of Poles, Dutch, French, Italians, and Swiss. Nothing written next to any of the names proved helpful.

As was the case with all ships entering the harbor, the ship's medical staff was responsible for granting medical clearance to the first- and second-class passengers. It was the responsibility of the medical staff on the island to examine and grant clearance to all the passengers traveling in steerage. Dr. White had assured Alexander that all the females in steerage had already been examined by the Ellis Island medical staff, who concluded that none could possibly have given birth on board.

Alexander understood his responsibility to find options to present to the Board of Special Inquiry so they could make an informed decision that best served the interests of the child and the nation. Yet he had spent three hours doing nothing to accomplish this.

At any moment, a messenger from the board would knock on his office door, arriving to escort him to the Great Hall and the small courtroom-like office adjacent to the hall where the board heard special cases. His panic grew with each passing second. The clock on the wall opposite his desk seized his attention. Alexander felt its accusing, mocking ticks as the hands proceeded further around its face.

There was one option he entertained immediately upon learning of the child, but he knew from experience with the board that it would be rejected. He had offered to raise as his own one or two of twelve Russian orphans who had arrived two years earlier. The children had been orphaned as a result of various Russian pogroms. His daughter, Ruth, had just turned two, and Eli was approaching his first birthday. Surely, Alexander had thought, the board would recognize the value of allowing some of these children to be raised in a loving home rather than being placed in one of the city's orphanages.

Alexander cringed as he recalled the four-member board's reaction to his suggestion. Arrangements had previously been made to send the children to New York's Foundling Hospital and wait for adoption. Many had already been claimed by families in the Midwest, and these children were set to ride the orphan train within a month of arriving at Ellis Island. Alexander's suggestion was seen as an affront to the board's authority and the protocol the island must follow in relation to other governing authorities in the city and nation. He was certain that the board would seek to continue this cooperative spirit, and any options he presented must also.

Again, he looked at the clock.

"It would have never worked," Alexander said under his breath as he recalled the Russian orphans. Although Ruth was a perfect daughter, the perfect first child, Eli was a challenge. To have two other children in their small home would have been unfair to his wife, Sarah. And now she was expecting again. Bringing this new orphaned child into their home was not possible.

He reached for the large framed picture of his family on his desk. Smiling, he traced his wife's face gently with his finger on the glass frame. He raised his hand from the glass, kissed it once and touched the top of Ruth's head, kissed it a second time and touched Eli.

Placing the picture of his family back on the desk, he sighed and again glanced at the clock, this time being drawn by the picture next to it on the wall. He rose from his chair, walked to the picture, and bent his knees slightly so he was at eye level with the photograph. Unlike the family portrait on his desk, it was not a professional photo. It had been taken four years earlier, just prior to meeting Sarah. In it, Alexander stood with three friends garbed in dusted suspenders, tools hanging from pockets, each with his arm around the shoulder of the friend next to him. Thomas Kemp, his college roommate, was on the far left, his smile the largest of the four. Next to Thomas was Elias, the only family man amongst them. Though he was smiling in the picture, it was a sensible smile, as if saying, "These guys are good chaps, but we've a job to get to." Next to Elias was Nathaniel, the eldest of the four, the most serious, and the one to whom Alexander had the most difficulty relating. In the picture, behind the friends stood an imposing circular steel structure, the likes the world had never seen prior to the Chicago World's Fair.

The structure had been designed by George Washington Ferris, an engineer from Pittsburgh. The fair's governing body had given their blessing and ordered Ferris to complete his project by the time the fair opened in May 1893. The chief architect and designer of the fair, its exhibits, and buildings was Chicago's own Daniel Burnham. The task was immense, and the greatest fear shared by all involved was their inability to fulfill the national expectation that they introduce something of equal or greater grandeur than the Eiffel Tower, introduced at the previous world's fair in Paris. Alexander and his friends had heard rumors of potential projects, some bordering on the ridiculous. One such idea was to build a tower that reached five hundred feet taller than Eiffel, constructed of timber, with a log cabin resting on top.

Stories such as this provided some relief to the constant stress workers at the fair site shared. The frequent setbacks that occurred prior to the fair's scheduled opening seemed apocalyptic. In the spring of '91, an abnormally wet April and May created such a clog of mud that construction of the fair's buildings could not begin until July. In December of the same year, four construction workers died from fractured skulls at two of the construction sites. The nation's economy was struggling as banks and companies failed. Adversity grew into the next year: windstorms destroyed buildings, torrential rain created sewage spills from the Chicago River, and the roof of a completed building collapsed from heavy snowfall.

With each new catastrophe, the pressure to complete the exhibits was keenly felt. Alexander, Thomas, Elias, and Nathaniel found amongst themselves a sanctuary in which they excelled. Each friend possessed a unique set of skills that enabled them to stick together from one construction site to the next as the managers recognized the value they brought as a team. Elias had built his own home and started a side business in which he purchased land, built homes in the growing suburbs, and sold them. Though successful at first, Elias was forced by the struggling economy to earn additional income by working as a carpenter at the fair. Thomas was a college-educated engineer. When a tool was not working properly, or a measurement was not exact, or a more efficient way of accomplishing a task was needed, Thomas solved the problem. Nathaniel was the strongest among the four, the most resilient, the most stubborn. He led by example and would not tolerate workers he felt were not contributing to the team.

Although he was a recent graduate from Northwestern, Alexander felt disillusioned with his prospects, unsure how to best utilize his economics degree. He considered returning to his parents' farm in Iowa, but his father seemed to have higher expectations for his youngest child. Alexander's five older brothers had proven capable of maintaining the farm and increasing the production of crops. Of what value would he be in returning? When he learned of Thomas's plan to work at the fair, he followed.

When he and Thomas reported for work their first day, all seemed desolate. Burnham and his staff had chosen Jackson Park as the ideal location—just outside the city, but close to the transportation network of Chicago. There were isolated groups of oak, plum, and willow trees, but the dominating features of the land were emptiness, ugliness, and mud. Within a few weeks, this same land was scattered with six barn-sized dredges, thousands of men armed with shovels and filling wheelbarrows with mud and gravel, horse-drawn graders scraping the landscape, burning piles of leaves, and bright white stakes stuck in the ground, marking the future sites of the fair's exhibit buildings. Once the construction began, Thomas and Alexander worked at the Manufactures and Liberal Arts Building—the largest and most prominent of the fair's structures. It was here that they met Nathaniel and Elias. Once the Manufactures Building was complete, the four traveled together. From there, they went to work at the Mines and Mining Building, then the Electricity Building, and finally, assisted the engineer from Pittsburgh to complete his large circular steel creation.

Although the official dedication of the fair took place in October of '92, the grand opening was scheduled for May 1. As the opening drew near, it became clear that the steel-wheeled carnival ride would not be ready. The four friends worked around the clock for the next month, and during the first week of June, thirty-six cars were attached to a wheel that was 264 feet in circumference. When the wheel first began to turn, powered by steam boilers several hundred feet away, a thunderous, creaking rasp startled the workers. Alexander turned to his friends, looking for assurance that there was nothing to fear. He sensed they shared his sentiment that the whole structure was on the verge of collapse. But the wheel turned, the sound faded, and then the wheel turned freely with no sound and with a grace that seemed to defy engineering logic. After several seconds of silence, cheering rose among the workers. Their clapping, dancing, and jumping reached to the sky as they pointed to the marvel before them. Once the wheel had made several revolutions, the operators stopped it momentarily, giving the workers a window of opportunity to jump aboard and be the first to ride. Alexander, Nathaniel, Elias, and Thomas climbed into one of the cars.

Gazing at the photo, Alexander remembered how his heart raced when the car climbed high into the darkening sky. When it reached its apex, with the sun's rays still strong enough to reflect off the waters of Lake Michigan and the man-made waterways meandering through the fairgrounds, Alex and his friends were silent, their cheering and shouting and laughing that had filled the car as they ascended to the top ended. Though the fair had been open for a month, they had been so consumed with their work, they had yet to walk the grounds. The buildings seemed to shine. The grounds were pristine, and emerald green burst from all corners, a benefit of the torrential rains earlier in the year. Boats and shrubs and trees danced with the children who raced from exhibit to exhibit, pulling their parents by the arm. Until that moment, Alexander had not realized what he helped create—a paradise, a playground, a diversion for all those who entered the fair's gates.

For the next five months, Alexander walked the streets of the fair daily. He was sure that during the rest of his days he would never contribute to something that brought so much joy to his fellow man. His greatest happiness was witnessing children discover something new—their eyes aglow, fingers pointing with excitement at some object, bodies jumping in place. He heard them begging their parents or older sibling to take them to the Algerian bazaar, the Great White Horse Inn, Germany's Krupp Monster, the chocolate Venus de Milo, the Ferris wheel, or Buffalo Bill's

Wild West show just outside the fairgrounds. He remembered how his heart melted the day he heard a small girl tell her father, "This is the best day of my life."

He reached for the picture and removed it from the nail from which it hung. Alexander shook his head—how was it that only four years ago he had stood arm in arm with his friends? How had so much happened since those glorious days? How had he lost touch with these three men who meant so much to him? He wondered what each might suggest in this predicament he now faced. What advice might each give? When they were working the fair, Alexander had no family or responsibilities to which he must go in the evening, and neither did Thomas or Nathan, so they stayed up late into the night after a fifteen-hour workday, discussing philosophy, politics, theology, their dreams. He trusted them and had often wished they lived closer so he could ask their advice or just have a cup of coffee with them at the corner café. But Elias was raising his three boys in Chicago, and his construction business was once again thriving. Nathaniel had returned to the Badlands in Dakota Territory. Thomas had returned to college, received a second degree in history, and become a Xaverian Brother, serving the diocese of Baltimore at St. Mary's reform school. Elias was a thousand miles away. He had no idea where Nathan may be—perhaps still in Dakota, maybe further west. Only Thomas was nearby.

A knock on the door forced Alexander back to reality. "Come in," he invited.

"Mr. Chalmers," a young page announced, "the board is waiting."

Alexander placed the picture of his friends back onto the wall and walked back to his desk, picking up the stack of papers he received from Dr. White three hours earlier. Though he had grown familiar with the case of the nameless orphan, he was not prepared with options to present to the board. As he walked back toward the door, he quickly turned, remembering the pending files from the previous day that were resting on the far-right corner of his desk. He grabbed them with his right hand, finding humor that he easily lifted the ten files with the strength of several fingers while he struggled to brace the pages from the orphan case between his left arm and hip. Fearing that he might soon drop all the pages, he set the other cases back on the desk, carefully placed the orphan case next to them, then placed the ten files on top of the large stack.

Feeling he securely held the papers, he walked through the doorway and nodded to the young man who closed the door behind them. As they exited the building, the young page sped past Alexander, rushing off to his next task.

"Mr. Edwards," Alexander called out, "hold on, please."

Edwards stopped and turned. "Yes, sir? Would you like me to carry those?" he asked, pointing at the folders, his face twisted with wrinkles of anxiety that Alexander felt did not belong on someone his age.

Alexander caught up to him. "Edwards?" he began. "You arrived this morning—yes?"

"Yes, sir."

"You've been to the room?"

Edwards nodded again. "Yes, Mr. Chalmers."

Alexander caught up to the page. "Who's on the bench?"

Edwards looked up toward the sky and pressed his eyes shut, appearing to force his mind to remember who formed the four-member Board of Special Inquiry that morning.

"Oxley . . . ," he started. "Jarret . . . , Francis, and . . . and Conners."

Alexander nodded and smiled. He felt some relief and was pleased. The four men were not the harshest amongst those currently serving on the board. Each had at some point served as an officer, and each had in the past shown compassion toward those on whom they passed judgment.

"Thank you, Edwards."

The young man looked at Alexander as if seeking permission to leave. Alexander grinned. "Have a nice weekend, Edwards," he shouted as he watched the page race back toward the Great Hall.

As he approached the entrance to the hall, he glanced to his right and could see a ship making its way toward the harbor. It was near enough that he recognized the Norwegian flag waving at the rear, the red-and-black smokestack, and the three distinctive masts of the *Norge*. Alexander challenged himself to recognize ships, creating a game to see how quickly he could name the ships as they approached. The *Norge* was the first to enter that day—the first to enter after the *Noordland* had docked the previous evening.

Losing himself in a moment of pride for recognizing the Norwegian ship, he almost collided with some fellow employees who had just exited the Great Hall. Among them was Edwards, still wearing his look of anxiety.

"Mr. Chalmers," he said, "the commissioner would like you to visit his office."

This was not a welcome revelation, and Alexander felt his face frowning.

Edwards reached out toward the files Alexander held. "He asked me to carry these for you."

Alexander nodded, handing the stack of papers to Edwards, then followed the page toward the commissioner's office.

He pressed his lips together. Although he had worked for three years on the island and had grown to recognize that particular cases required delicacy, he never felt comfortable giving preferential treatment to one immigrant. Still, he was an employee of the state and was obligated to do as he was told. It was a balancing act, a thin gray line that he pushed and tested as much as he was able, making it his priority to serve the newcomers as best he could. He used as many resources as were available but was frustrated that often these resources were held back by those with more authority.

They reached the commissioner's office. Edwards knocked on the door, just under the name plate with the commissioner's name: Dr. Joseph H. Senner.

"Enter," a voice from inside invited.

Alexander turned the knob since Edwards still embraced the stack of papers with both arms.

"Officer Chalmers," the commissioner announced playfully, "we've got a situation."

"Yes, sir."

Dr. Senner turned to face the young page. "Thank you, Master Edwards. You did well. Place those on the desk and report back to the board."

Edwards took several quick steps toward the commissioner's desk, placed the papers down, and scurried back to the office entrance.

Senner sat in his large reclining chair and motioned with his arm, inviting Alexander to sit in one of the two chairs on the other side of his desk.

"Alex," Dr. Senner began, "we've guests in the Hearing Room that require special attention. We must tread lightly."

Alexander nodded, fairly confident that the guests to whom the commissioner referred were newspapermen. The past decade had produced a sordid type of symbiotic relationship between the island's employees and

New York's journalistic profession. There were periods when the New York newspapers praised the work of the immigration inspection officers, the medical staff, and the Board of Special Inquiry. But occasionally an article would appear in the *Sun* or the *Tribune* or the *Times* that subtly questioned the ease with which immigrants entered the country. Then several months or even weeks later, another reporter from a different newspaper would suggest that the medical staff was cruel and harsh, unjustly denying entrance into the country because of a minor ailment.

But Alexander observed his coworkers with the cynical perspective he had learned during his college years. He considered himself to be a good judge of character, and from his perspective, the workers on Ellis Island were diligent in their service to the nation and their future fellow citizens. Their service had not changed, as was sometimes suggested by the local reporters. They were as faithful today as they were yesterday and would prove to be tomorrow.

Senner continued. "We must be extra cautious with the proceedings regarding the child from the *Noordland*."

Alexander nodded. "That is why the papers will remain here?" He phrased it almost as though it were not a question but a fact—a strategy with which he agreed.

"That is correct."

"Any indication as to why they decided to come today?"

"It's the volume of ships," Senner answered. "Seven ships on the seventh, three more on the eighth, five over the next two days, including the *Noordland,* and already the *Norge* arrives this morning. They can see them approach through the harbor from their perches in Manhattan. They're as predictable as the seasons. They figure that out of all these newcomers, there must be at least one or two sensational, heartwarming stories to help sell more of their papers."

It warmed Alexander to hear his superior speak like this. It meant that as much as Senner might be accused of having political aspirations, of using his position as a stepping stone to a more prominent role, he did not look kindly on anything or anyone who interrupted the service provided by those he managed.

"We will proceed as normal. The board has a docket full of cases. Feel free to take those in with you." Dr. Senner pointed at the ten thin files resting atop the *Noordland* file.

Senner continued. "We don't want to raise any suspicion that some extraordinary case is to be decided. We're hoping that their editors will provide transportation back to Battery Park before 4:30, but if not, we will need you to stay over the weekend to present the case to the board on Saturday morning."

Alexander saw the determination with which the commissioner spoke. The situation was presented as though there were no options. Either the reporters would leave prior to the ferry's final departure, thus enabling the board to deliberate over the orphan's fate without any threat of the child's story becoming sensationalized, or the entire board as well as Alexander would spend the weekend away from family.

Alexander sighed. He lowered his head involuntarily, thinking of Sarah and the children, but quickly raised it, conscious of the need to show solidarity. "Yes, sir." Alexander answered. "I understand."

Despite his verbal agreement with Senner's request, Alexander wondered why they could not use the island's own ferry to get back to Manhattan after the regular ferry had departed.

"We have arranged for telegrams to be sent to your family from Battery Park in case the need arises."

"Yes, sir."

"Thank you, Alex." The commissioner stood and extended his hand.

Alex reached for the ten thin files, quickly stood, and shook Senner's hand.

"And Alex," the commissioner added, "you and the board will decide. You are the officer that is best capable of helping the child. I will not interfere or question your decision."

Alexander smiled, grateful for Senner's confidence. He waited for some sign that he could leave.

Senner walked to Alex's side, put his arm around his shoulder, and walked with him to the door. "Remember," he whispered, "where there are no wounded, there are no vultures waiting to feed. And where there are no vultures, the wounded still have hope."

Alex winced and quickly tried to hide the wince, feeling uncomfortable with Dr. Senner's philosophizing over the fate of the child.

* * *

Worn wooden benches creaked and whined, and the sounds echoed throughout the room. Old men, expressions fraught with uncertainty, sat amongst young men, eyes alive with anticipation. Mothers cradled infants, and young children fended off siblings, chasing one another through rows filled with anxious strangers dressed in multicolored fabrics—wool and cotton, striped and checkered, light and dark.

Alexander sat in the last row next to a large Cossack man wearing a blue tunic, blue trousers with crimson stripes, and a tall crimson fleece shako atop his head. He looked somber and determined, his arms crossed over his chest as though ready to go into battle. Alexander imagined what fears plagued the Cossack. What was it about this new land that caused the greatest anxiety? After all the trials he had overcome, leaving his homeland and family, now he was faced with the threat of being placed back on a ship and returned to the other side of the Atlantic.

He had seen the list of ships recently entering New York Harbor— fifteen ships within the past four days. Sitting in the benches, Alexander began to deduce on which ship each detainee had arrived. There were several families huddled near the center of the room, wearing wooden

29

shoes, but since none of the recently arrived ships had originated from Amsterdam, he figured the Dutch families must have come on one of the three ships from Bremen. He noticed several women with dark olive skin and determined they must have arrived on one of the two ships from Naples. A dark-skinned man dressed in white, with a white turban, was certain to be from northern Africa or the Middle East. Alexander also concluded he must have boarded somewhere in Italy.

And then there was this infant, this nameless child, whom Alexander had yet to meet, whose future had been entrusted into his care. The child's mother had boarded in Antwerp. This was perhaps the only fact in the case—all else was conjecture. Since the *Noordland* made no port stops on its journey to America, there could be no other port from which she boarded. She must have been determined to find a way to stow passage on a ship notoriously unfriendly to stowaways. Or maybe, Alexander considered, she was desperate—desperate enough to attempt the improbable. Although she succeeded in getting aboard the *Noordland*, and although she remained incognito for most of the journey, and even though she gave birth to a healthy child, still, she decided to end her life.

Alexander's attention was drawn to the front of the room where a young man was pleading in German, through an interpreter, motioning to what appeared to be his young family sitting on the first bench. Alexander could not let himself get emotionally involved in a case that was not his own. Soon he would be beckoned by the board to present the cases he had not looked at for almost twenty-four hours. He glanced down and opened the top file, hoping to reacquaint himself quickly with each of the ten cases.

An hour passed. And another. The board dismissed for lunch.

Alexander remained seated, studying his files.

When the board reentered an hour later, he looked up and noticed for the first time the string of reporters from New York's leading newspapers following in their wake and sitting together near the front left corner. There were five, each adorned with that expression Alexander learned to disdain— an eager hope to learn of another human's suffering.

Alex studied the face of each board member as they sat at the long wooden desk several feet from the benches of immigrants. The board's desk was elevated several feet above the floor and separated from the rest of the Hearing Room by a swinging wooden gate that gave the room a feel of American jurisprudence. The board consisted of the three members, who would decide each case, and the secretary, who took minutes of the proceedings.

Oxley, the senior board member, quickly turned his head to the rear of the room and looked at Alexander. He appeared to be waiting for Alexander to give some signal. Conscious of the discussion he had earlier with Dr. Senner, Alexander froze, uncertain how his reaction might be interpreted by any of the reporters observing him. He decided a nod would not be wise, and a wink would be too subtle, so he smiled as if to say, "Hello, Ox. Nice to see you today." Oxley nodded in return. Alexander returned to studying the last of the ten files, waiting about a minute before glancing at the reporters to see if the exchange between he and Oxley had raised any suspicion. Based upon the five reporters' banter amongst themselves, it did not appear he had been discovered.

Another hour passed. Still, Alexander sat, waiting.

Two of the five reporters had left about thirty minutes earlier. It was almost three o'clock, and the three remaining journalists were frantically writing notes. The benches had been full when Alexander entered around ten and had emptied just before the board dismissed for lunch. They were full again within minutes after lunch, then emptied again. And still, the board had heard none of Alexander's cases. Finally, just after three o'clock, several immigrants Alexander recognized were led into the room by Edwards, the young page who had assisted Alexander earlier.

An unexpected rush of shame filled Alexander as he watched Edwards walk to Oxley, hand him several folders, then rush back out into the Great Hall. He did not know and had never even bothered to ask Edwards's first name. This young man, so full of anxiety and desire to please his superiors, played an integral role in the life of the island. He was the blood in the veins, delivering messages from one side of the island to the other, carrying the fates of immigrants in his hands as he sped from one task to the next. And yet Alexander had never spoken to him about anything outside of his duties.

This often happened just prior to his appearing before the board: something would catch his attention, distracting him from a task, maybe something of great importance, but certainly not as important as his duty to the new arrivals.

"Officer Chalmers," Oxley called out. "Please join us in front." Oxley looked up, smiled, and motioned to the chair just to the right and a little behind the secretary.

"Leading off," Oxley began, "case number 53215."

Alexander appreciated Oxley—he was an avid baseball fan, and they often discussed current events on the field while at lunch in the employee cafeteria. Normally, with the other officers, Oxley was formal and would introduce each case as "first on the docket" or "next on the docket," but the phrases "leading off" and "batting second" were reserved for cases Alexander presented.

Alexander stood and handed case number 53215 to the secretary. He was pleased that Oxley and the board decided to begin with this particular case. Alexander had been working on it for almost two weeks and felt he at last had enough supporting documentation to help the board make a final decision. The Bender family had arrived from Germany with no money. The father, Dietrich, had wounded his ankle on the ship while crossing the Atlantic and also had a horrible cough, causing the medical staff to suspect tuberculosis or worse. Both the medical team and the examining immigration officer placed the dreaded letters *SI* next to each family member's name, designating that the Board of Special Inquiry would decide their fate.

Alexander remained standing as he spoke. He asked Dietrich Bender to stand, reintroduced him to the board, then invited him to sit.

"As you are aware," Alexander began, "the minutes from last week's proceedings indicate Mr. Bender's health has improved, and he no longer has a cough. Though he still limps because of his injured ankle, the swelling has decreased, and the medical staff has confirmed that no bones are broken."

Alexander paused and glanced at the board, attempting to get some indication as to how they may respond to his next piece of evidence. "Furthermore," he continued, "with regard to the financial stature of the Bender family, I have received letters from Mr. Bender's cousin and brother-in-law, both residing in Boston, stating that Mr. Bender is a highly skilled carpenter, and they have procured employment opportunities on his behalf. Mr. Bender's cousin is a professor at Harvard University and has a flourishing law practice. He has two homes, one which the family occupies for vacations in Newburyport, just north of the city. His cousin, as you can see from his signed affidavit, has guaranteed that he will allow Mr. Bender and his family to reside in the Newburyport home until he has saved sufficient funds to rent or purchase his own residence."

Alexander was finished. He had made no further progress on the case. He ground his teeth silently, fearing that his failure to garner more guarantees of the Bender family not becoming a strain on the American public would cause the board to send them back to Germany.

A resounding thump echoed through the room as the secretary marked case number 53215 as "Approved Entry."

Alexander sighed as he read the bold red ink just under Bender's case number.

"That took less than five minutes," Alexander thought to himself. He hoped the nine remaining cases could be decided just as quickly.

The three reporters remained seated on their bench in the Hearing Room, still writing, still appearing eager to hear a case that could capture their readers' imaginations. It was almost four o'clock. The last ferry for Battery Park would leave in thirty minutes. The chances of him being able to make it were not good.

By 4:20, nine of Alexander's ten files had been decided. The board was making quick work of the cases, approving all but one. Still, the three reporters remained.

Alexander opened the tenth case, and just as he was about to begin, he noticed all three reporters simultaneously look at their watches, scuttle their papers into their satchels, and rush through the doors into the Great Hall's main entrance.

The board looked at Alexander. Alexander turned and looked behind him. Alone, seated in the third bench, was the subject of Alexander's final case. He turned back around when he heard the thump of the secretary's stamp. Without his speaking a word, the secretary had stamped "Approved Entry."

"Now what?" Alexander muttered. He studied Oxley, hoping for them to make one last quick decision for the day.

Oxley was in the midst of gathering his papers and placing them in his large briefcase. "Alexander." Oxley sighed. "We have rooms reserved at Dr. White's home. We will see you tomorrow morning."

The board left, leaving Alexander alone. He fell to his chair and lowered his head, bracing it with a hand on either side of his face. He absorbed the reality that he would not see his family for two or three days. Wallowed in the certainty of boredom he would endure over the weekend, he was still uncertain what he would present as options when the board reconvened the next morning.

He heard a knock on the doors separating the Great Hall from the Hearing Room. Peering through the square glass window of the door, he recognized Dr. White. His friend smiled, then pushed the door open.

He was carrying a bassinet. Wrapped inside a thick white blanket, the child was asleep.

Alexander stood and walked toward his friend.

Dr. White gently lowered the child onto the top of the desk.

Alexander tilted his head and studied the child. "This is he?"

"It is," the doctor answered.

Unconsciously, Alexander smiled. The child rested peacefully. How could he be aware of the cards he had been dealt? When would he grow to know the misfortune bestowed upon him? Alexander stopped smiling. He placed his hands in his pockets, then took them out of his pockets, then crossed his arms, then looked at Dr. White.

"I have no idea, Joseph," Alexander confessed. "I have no idea how to serve this child's best interest. Who am I to decide his fate?"

"Alex, how many cases have you overseen? How many have you resolved?"

Alexander raised his hand. "This is different. The child is helpless. Has nobody. The one person who should care for him deserted him hours after she gave birth . . . and . . . and we don't know why. We don't—I don't even know where to start."

The doctor walked closer to Alexander and placed both hands on his shoulders. "You've thought of options?" he asked.

"I don't feel anything will bring this child anything but sorrow. Regardless of what we decide."

"Sit down, Alexander," the doctor requested.

The doctor's tone was soft, but based upon the expression Alexander read on his friend's face, he interpreted it as an order.

"Sit. I have something to show you."

Alexander obediently sat on the front bench.

"You say, 'Whatever we do can only bring the child sorrow'?"

The doctor waited for some sign of response from Alexander.

"That's what you said just now—correct?"

Alexander shrugged, agreeing with his friend.

The doctor continued. "What if we could ensure the child has sufficient funds for an education? If we could somehow guarantee that if he makes it safely to his eighteenth birthday, with enough education to be accepted into a reputable college or university, he could pay for this education?"

A college education? Alexander thought. Of what relevance was an education to the decision they now faced? Of what value was the promise of college to finding this child a safe place to survive and grow through his formative years?

"Listen, Alex. Your job is to find a place that will help this child thrive for sixteen, seventeen years . . . and after that?" The doctor paused, reached into his jacket's inner pocket, and held up a small felt bag with drawstrings.

"Two possessions this child was given by his mother," the doctor continued. "The child was found in this blanket by the *Noordland*'s nightwatchman."

Alexander looked into the bassinet, studying more closely the blanket wrapped tightly around the child. He reached inside and touched it, feeling the warmth of the child and the scratch of the blanket's thick wool. The whiteness of the fabric was accentuated by the brown embroidered perimeter extending several inches inward from each edge. In the midst of the blanket there was writing, brown letters stitched into the body of white.

Its message was illegible, not only because the letters disappeared somewhere under the child's body, but also because the writing appeared Cyrillic.

Alexander placed his hand under the child's nose and felt the warm exhale of air, just as he had when his daughter and son were born.

"The bag from your jacket? This is the child's second inheritance you spoke of?"

"Open your hand," the doctor invited.

Alexander walked closer to his friend and held out his right hand.

The doctor stepped forward, gently loosened the small bag's drawstrings, held it just above Alexander's palm, and emptied the contents.

Three diamonds tumbled from the bag into Alexander's hand.

The light in the room danced on the stones.

The feel, the weight, the color were unmistakable.

At first glance, he knew the stones were of greater value than anything he had ever held before or likely would ever hold again.

* * *

Two hours after Alexander had presented his case to the board, he sent a telegraph message to inquire whether he could proceed with the board's approved action.

Two hours had passed since Alexander sent the message, and he had yet to receive a response.

The installation of telegraph cables connecting the city with the island had been completed that morning, just as Alexander had been presenting his case before the board. He hoped the installation had succeeded, that the engineers had completed their tests, that the wiring was intact, and that the message he sent to Baltimore had been received.

The events of the morning were a pleasant surprise. All had gone better than he could have hoped. Dr. White allowed Alexander and the three board members to sleep in his children's bedrooms. The children welcomed the opportunity to sleep under a tent on their home's front lawn, the New York skyline shining in the distance. A breakfast of scrambled eggs, sausages, toast, orange juice, and coffee was prepared and served by Mrs. White and her eldest daughter. Alexander had anticipated an effort-filled ordeal, searching for options of where to settle the *Noordland*'s child, and fearful that the options he suggested would not be accepted.

Because it was the weekend, the Hearing Room had lost some of its mystique. The lack of the usual crowd of immigrants waiting for their hearings created an absence of formality, making the room feel strange and foreign. The grandeur that usually dominated proceedings was gone.

The board immediately invited Alexander to present the case. The air of cordiality eased much of his apprehension. He opened with the suggestion of finding a home for the child in the West. This would require several days or weeks of searching for a home, accompanying the child on an orphan train, and ensuring that the adopting family was a good match. After Alexander presented this option, the board remained silent, their eyes clearly inviting Alexander to continue with a more viable alternative.

The next option he presented was taking the child to New York's Foundling Hospital. From there, the staff could find a home for the child in the West.

Again, the board was silent.

Next, Alexander listed orphanages in Manhattan, Brooklyn, Long Island, and New Jersey to which the island had sent orphans in the past. The difference was that these orphans had all arrived with no surprise. The officers, the board, and the commissioner were aware long in advance of their landing at the immigration station.

Once more, the board remained silent.

Oxley shuffled papers, and for the first time, Alexander perceived some irritation.

He hadn't put much effort or passion into the previous alternatives, hoping the board would see his next idea as the best alternative. He knew of their desire to keep the child hidden from discovery by the New York press. He knew that they, like he, desired to find a place in which the child could have a reasonable chance to thrive. He knew the urgency of resolving the matter.

"There is an orphanage in the outskirts of Baltimore," he told the board. "St. Mary's."

When he said these few words, all four members raised their heads, their eyes widened, and subtle smiles appeared simultaneously on each face.

Alexander continued. "I have a college friend who is a Xaverian Brother and serves as a teacher at St. Mary's Industrial School for Boys. I have not contacted him, but if we decide on this course, the child could attend the school once he is of age and thereby get an education and have a chance to enter adulthood with skills that could sustain him through life."

Oxley reached for his gavel and ceremoniously hammered the desk. "Confirm with your friend, complete the required forms, prepare the birth certificate, and go."

These were the events Alexander pondered while waiting for the response from his friend over the telegraph.

Dr. Senner had rewarded the board for their quick decision by chartering a ferry to Manhattan. Alexander, however, still had work to accomplish: confirm the child would be welcomed at St. Mary's and complete the paperwork, including the birth certificate, which required naming the child.

Best case scenario would be for his friend Thomas and his superiors to agree with the board's recommendation and accept the child. There was, however, the likelihood of them delaying making a decision, or worse, denying the child entrance into the orphanage. Alexander closed his eyes and dug his fingers into his forehead, pushing to relieve the pounding turmoil and anxiety.

Several messages had been received by the telegraph clerk just after twelve o'clock. None were from Thomas. The machine's clicking became more frequent. It appeared word was beginning to spread on the mainland that the island now had a working telegraph. Still, no messages were received from Baltimore.

Alexander left the telegraph office at two o'clock, just in time to see another ship pass underneath the Brooklyn Bridge. Within minutes he recognized it as a ship from Hamburg—the *Persia*. On a normal day he would imagine some of the stories the ship carried, but the *Noordland*'s child dominated his thinking. Would Thomas and the brothers at St. Mary's accept the child? Would the child be sufficiently nurtured within their care? And then the particulars began to overwhelm him: the documents he needed to complete, the diamonds about which only he and Dr. White knew, the filing of a birth certificate.

He felt a desperate urge to see the infant and hoped that just by seeing him rest, he may receive some inspiration in naming the child. He walked to the hospital, entered the nursery, and pulled a chair next to the crib in which the child was sleeping.

Draped across one side of the crib was the wool blanket. The brown lettering was clear to view, but impossible to read:

Принцесса Шут выбрала его

проявить свою злобу

The letters were near the far-right side of the blanket, directly to the right of an intricately stitched home or farmhouse. The image was large and comprised the center of the blanket. The portrayal of the structure was made of a variety of materials. Burnt red fabric had been used to represent bricks, dark green fabric for the roof, and bright yellow fabric for the windows. A brown fabric was used for the doors. On both ends of the structure were two tall, thin chimneys, also made of the burnt red fabric.

The artisan who created the blanket was clearly skilled. The colors were deep, the stitching snug. The angles and corners and dimensions of the farmhouse transported Alexander momentarily into another place, somewhere perhaps back in the Midwest, closer to his family, closer to his childhood, closer to a reality that carried less responsibility. His years in Iowa had been full of blessed interactions with family, neighbors, and friends. He wondered if this child would ever have similar moments of happiness.

When the doctor first showed him the blanket, Alexander did not think much of it—it was just something to keep the child warm, one meager piece of his legacy left by his mother. But the diamonds were another matter. Dr. White assured Alexander that nobody on the medical staff knew about the gems, nor did anyone on the ship, or any other employee on the island. No one except the two of them. How, Alexander thought, had they gone unnoticed until Dr. White examined the child?

"The strings of the bag were tightly wrapped in a knot," the doctor had explained. "And sewn into the interior of the blanket, behind one of the chimneys."

Alexander stood from his chair and walked to the blanket. He touched each of the chimneys on the blanket's surface, examining them, trying to determine how three diamonds could be kept secret from the ship's medical crew. The fabric stitched onto the blanket was raised, supported by padding underneath, elevating the farmhouse above the surface of the wool. Perhaps, Alexander surmised, the diamonds could remain hidden amidst the padding in the blanket's stitching. The doctor had discovered the stones just before he was about to throw the blanket toward the laundry basket in the nursery. He felt something solid in the midst of the billowy fabric. Examining the blanket closer, he isolated the hard objects, cut into the chimney, extracted the diamonds, sewed the tear, and placed the blanket into the laundry.

Standing above the blanket, Alexander moved his hand across the wool, his fingers dancing through the thick fabric. The child woke, and seeing this stranger before him rubbing his comforter did not seem to disturb him. Actually, it appeared to Alexander that the child was happy for a visit and almost smiled before wiggling and boxing his arms in the air.

Alexander reached down, embraced the child to his chest, and quickly discovered he needed a change. The room was empty—the nurses on duty had left moments earlier to care for newly arriving patients. Alexander shrugged, welcoming the tangible opportunity to serve the child.

After replacing the diaper, Alexander rocked the child to sleep, laid him in the crib, and waited for one of the nurses to return before he walked to Dr. White's home, still no closer to coming up with a name.

He ate dinner, slept upstairs in one of Dr. White's children's rooms, woke Sunday morning, and headed straight to the telegraph office.

Still no response from Thomas.

No ships arrived on Sunday.

No telegram arrived.

END OF THE BEGINNING

On Monday Alexander returned to his office and served in the Great Hall, examining the immigrants who had arrived that morning. It was something he had not done in over a year since he received a promotion, but the routine and constant flow of immigrants helped keep his mind off the fact that he still had received no response from Baltimore.

At noon, Alexander sent a message to his wife explaining that the circumstances that had kept him away over the weekend still required him to stay another night on the island.

After the last ferry for the day had left, Alexander went to the nursery and held the child, rocking him, setting him back into his crib, watching him sleep, seeking for inspiration that would help him come up with a name. The inspiration did not come.

Again, the ferry for Battery Park departed, and no response had been received from Thomas. Alexander left his office and walked to the Whites' home. Finally, just as the Whites were sitting for the meal, Edwards arrived to present a telegram. Alexander looked nervously at the page.

He reached for the telegram, retrieved his glasses from inside his jacket, looped them around his ears, and read:

* * *

Alexander convinced himself that he ought to be relieved—he ought to be sleeping. But it was just past midnight and he had much still to do. Seated behind his desk, watching the shadows from a candle's flame dance on the ceiling, he wondered if this was the best path.

He was certainly excited by the prospect that he'd see his family in just a few hours, but once he read the telegram from Thomas, the one thing that kept dancing through his mind was the responsibility for naming the child. It was the last hurdle. He had completed all the forms, all except the birth certificate.

He looked from the blank sheet of paper to the child wrapped in his wool blanket, sleeping peacefully in the bassinet Dr. White brought from the nursery and set in the chair opposite Alexander. He had asked if it were appropriate for him to keep the child from the nursery at night. The doctor assured him that at least one nurse would be on duty, ready to assist with burping, diaper changes, or feeding.

The absurdity of the stress Alexander felt over naming the child added to the anxiety. Of all that could possibly go wrong with the proceedings—the board not being cooperative, the press learning of the child, Thomas and the brothers at St. Mary's not being willing or able to accept him—all had gone rather well, considering the unique circumstances. And now, Alexander felt the greatest burden was his alone to bear.

He had considered naming the child Peter, or Ivan, or Alexander, any typical Russian name for a boy, since it appeared from the writing on the blanket that the child's origins might have been in Russia. One of the nurses whose parents had emigrated from Kiev read the words on the blanket for Alexander:

> *"Printsessa shut vybrala yego*
> *proyavit' svoyu zlobu."*

Then, she translated the words for him:

> "The jester's princess chose it,
> To manifest her spite."

The picture of the farmhouse on the blanket was beautiful. Even now, seeing the child wrapped in its warmth brought Alexander a feeling of comfort. Why, then, such strange words next to a picture of tranquility?

Of all the cases Alexander presided over, this was certainly the most challenging, strange, and unsettling. He was not confident the best decision had been made, and he was not certain that he had invested all he could to help the child. He was not optimistic that the child had much hope. Even if the diamonds found in the blanket were genuine and valuable, there were variables the child would need to navigate and overcome if he were to make use of the wealth.

Alexander recalled the stack of papers presented to him by Dr. White three days earlier. He had felt overwhelmed and had asked Master of the Universe for guidance. Now Alexander was worried again, as if he had encountered something new with which the Master could not assist, something over which the Master could not claim victory. Sarah would scold him for how easily he forgot. Alexander hung his head, recalling the times throughout his years that deliverance had emerged from dire events and blessings had arrived unexpectedly. Sarah was a constant reminder of the joy and blessing that could arrive unexpectedly.

It was only five years ago that his friend Nathaniel Marsh from the Chicago Fair had requested that Alexander accompany him to pick up his distant cousin, just arrived from Poland. She had lost her immediate family in a pogrom and had written to Nathan asking if he could sponsor her upon her arrival. Once Alexander saw her, heard her speak, observed her move, and witnessed her interactions with others, he felt an emptiness when he was no longer in her presence. The emptiness grew until the next time he was in her company.

He had been fascinated by Sarah that day on Ellis Island, but he recalled also being enthralled by the activity and energy he witnessed at the immigration station. He didn't feel qualified for any position but applied anyway. He was surprised when he moved so quickly through the interview process and was hired just one day after submitting his application.

Two miracles had emerged from his decision to accompany Nathan. Would any miracles emerge in the life of this child? Would Master look upon the child with mercy in the midst of all the faithless acts committed by those closest to the child? Could Master excuse any of the errors Alexander and his coworkers might have made in trying to serve the child's best interests?

Alexander looked down again at the blank paper and sighed. He reached for a pen—but quickly turned his head toward his office window when he caught the scent of burning wood.

He raced from his chair to the window and saw several night employees running from their sleeping quarters toward the Great Hall. Flames were dancing through most of the windows on the east side of the main building. Three men jumped to safety from the second floor as one worker ran toward the other side of the island, apparently to warn Dr. White and those in the hospital of the pending danger.

Alexander was on the far west side and knew he only had minutes to evacuate. He rushed to the bassinet and placed it on his desk. He gathered the strewn documents, stuffed them in a folder, and placed it in the bassinet next to the sleeping child. He set the picture of his family on the other side of the child and grabbed the bassinet. Before exiting his office, he set the bassinet on the floor, pulled the picture of his friends from the wall, and put it next to the picture of his family.

He looked behind him, certain it would be the last time he saw the items in his office, then raced out of the building into the courtyard.

Already, thick smoke filled the air, and Alexander joined the other employees as they ran toward the dock and boarded the *John G. Carlisle*. Looking around from coworker to immigrant, Alexander was grateful that the *Carlisle* remained docked overnight as policy. If it hadn't, it would have been at least an hour before any transport arrived to save them.

The ferry was already full. It appeared that all the people had been safely led on board. The hospital staff and Dr. White with his family were seated on the far end of the ferry. As they left the dock, a thunderous crash sounded from the Great Hall. Alexander looked back, seeing the Great Hall's roof collapse. Flames could be seen rising higher, with greater intensity.

Each face, it seemed, was filled with dazed gratitude. No one spoke. The only sounds were coughing, weeping, and waves dashing against the ferry's bows. Several minutes passed before sirens and motors of boats could be heard approaching from Manhattan. A fireboat raced past as someone on board shouted, asking if anyone was still on the island. One of the watchmen yelled that all had been evacuated.

Alexander looked down at the child. He was awake, his eyes fixed on Alexander as though seeking an explanation of what might be wrong. Alexander smiled and lightly patted the child on the side of his face, amazed that the child was not weeping. He felt he should hold him to help bring assurance that all would be okay. But as he considered this, he noticed Dr. White approaching.

"Alex." The doctor spoke in a whisper at first but then raised his voice over the noise of wind and waves. "It's good you were with the child. You have the documents?"

Alexander nodded. He felt some agenda was soon to be revealed.

"The chaos awaiting us." The doctor motioned toward Battery Park. "Full of police and reporters."

Alexander nodded. He sensed where this was headed.

The doctor reached into his coat pocket and held out the small bag with the diamonds. "Take them," he ordered, quickly grabbing Alexander's hand and placing the bag in his palm.

"They'll leave us on the north side. I've instructed the nurses to leave first, carrying the typhoid victim. We've placed the other patients on stretchers also, though none need it."

The doctor paused. "You understand?"

"Yes," Alexander answered.

"I've instructed them to rush to the south end of the park, anything to give the appearance that those on the stretchers are in grave circumstances."

Within minutes, the ferry would reach the pier. Shouts from the shore could be heard among neighing horses and sounds of carts approaching from the various streets that fed into the park.

Dr. White placed his hands on Alexander's shoulders. "After my staff has left, make sure you recognize no reporters on shore, then go. Take the child directly to Grand Central and wait for the first train to Baltimore. Board it, complete the documents, leave the child with your friend, and return to your family. I don't want to see you for a week."

"And Senner?" Alex asked. "The board?"

"I'll take responsibility. We've all been on the same page so far. Don't think it will be an issue."

* * *

All went as planned: the ferry docked, Dr. White's staff hurried the six stretchers with their patients to the south side of the park, and the reporters followed in their wake. Alexander left with the child, unnoticed, walked to Grand Central, and took the first southbound train.

He had hoped to sleep while waiting for the train to arrive but was unable to settle his nerves. Once he and the child were seated, a wave of calm washed over him, his eyes closed, and he slept. He woke when the train was running, the car full of passengers. He was unsure how far south they had traveled and was about to ask the lady across the aisle when he recognized the Philadelphia skyline approaching. Most of the passengers exited, and the car was mostly empty.

Across the aisle one row ahead of him, resting in the back pocket of the seat, was a folded newspaper. Alexander could just make out what appeared to be the baseball scores from the prior day's games.

He rose and looked up and down the aisle to make sure nobody suspected him of stealing someone else's newspaper. He grabbed it and returned to his seat.

He reached into his pocket and put on his glasses.

His Bridegrooms lost.

The Orioles won. And won big.

They defeated the team in Louisville 15–6.

Leadoff hitter, John McGraw, went 3–4, scoring two runs. Willie Keeler batted second and went 2–5, also scoring twice. The number three hitter, Hughie Jennings, only got one hit but somehow scored three runs.

Alexander raised his head. And wondered

Looking into the bassinet, he saw the child was awake. Alexander had purchased some milk while waiting for the train to arrive, and fortunately the baby's bottle had been in the bassinet when he rushed out of his office.

It was also fortunate that the child had only whimpered on several occasions and the filled bottle seemed to have appeased the infant's yearnings.

Alexander reached inside the bassinet and took out the envelope that held the child's documents. He opened it, reached inside for the birth certificate, then felt inside his pocket for his fountain pen.

Looking down at the box score again, he smiled.

"Wee Willie Keeler," Alexander announced softly, glancing at the child, then turning his attention to the paper before him. "May you be as agile, quick, and ingenious as he." Above the line of the birth certificate that read "First Name," he wrote, "William."

"John Mugsy McGraw." Alexander's smile grew wider. "May your determination, stubbornness, and desire lead you to success." And above the line that read "Middle Name," he wrote, "John."

"Hughie Jennings. May your energy, vociferousness, and leadership make you a blessing amongst those with whom you live."

As he wrote, Alexander whispered, "And your last name shall be Jennings."

Chapter 1

Horatio Nelson Jackson had been an ordinary man—at least, Thomas Kemp had not heard of him until recently. Now, sitting comfortably in a horse-drawn coach nearing the Scranton train station, Thomas was engrossed in the newspaper story about the previously unknown doctor from Vermont.

The report on Jackson read like a dime-store drama. Thomas turned the front page, eager to learn more of the Canadian-raised American citizen who graduated from the University of Vermont in 1893, began a medical practice in Burlington, and married the daughter of one of Vermont's wealthiest men. Without this wealth, Jackson likely would never have been able to partake in the adventure that had transformed him into a national hero within weeks.

Leaving San Francisco on the morning of May 23, Horatio and a friend set out east in a used Winton with the hopes of becoming the first to cross the nation in an automobile. Other adventure seekers had attempted the transcontinental trip, but all had failed. Many in the country were not even convinced that the new contraption could replace the trains, horses, and coaches that pushed the nation's economy forward.

But the headlines on Saturday, July 25, were brimming with anticipation as Horatio and his friend were just miles from New York City.

Crowds rushed in and out of Scranton Station's entrance as Thomas stepped from his coach. He dodged several men as they hurried onto the coach he had just left. He tugged the bill of his hat, greeting the men, but they did not respond. By the end of the day, he'd be wearing the long black cassock of the brothers that normally guaranteed expressions of respect, but today, wearing trousers and a tweed jacket, he looked like any other ordinary man. Again, he tipped his hat at others running past, but none acknowledged or reciprocated his gesture. He found the atmosphere amusing. Many were racing from one platform to the next, wearing eager smiles. Thomas thought briefly of changing his plans and joining the throng onto one of the eastbound trains, but he knew the other brothers were awaiting his arrival, eager to hear of his experiences away from St. Mary's over the past six years.

Once his train arrived, Thomas boarded and searched for a vacant seat that overlooked the platforms housing the eastbound trains. Another crowd rushed toward the next arriving train, racing from one car to the next, craning their necks, searching for any sign of room for one more passenger. From Thomas's perspective, it was a futile effort. Each car held more standing passengers than the lucky few who sat. It was difficult to tell where one body began and another ended. The mass of humanity in each window appeared as a large mass of fabric—brown and black trousers and jackets swaying and jarring as the crowd fought for their right to journey eastward.

Even in his train, Thomas sensed the pride among his fellow passengers and the crew. All seemed to walk tall and speak to one another as though they were playing some role in Jackson's cross-country adventure.

Thomas knew the celebration would be brief. Each day the papers carried a new story of optimism, something that captured the national imagination. Tomorrow the readers would grow weary of the story of a doctor from Vermont traveling across the country in an automobile. The populace would hunger for the press to report some new event that evidenced the unstoppable trajectory of where the country was headed. Even in the face of tragedy after the assassination of President McKinley, Roosevelt led the nation and kept the tide of progress moving forward. In January he had orchestrated the signing of a treaty with Colombia granting the United States the right to purchase land in Central America for the construction of a canal through the Isthmus of Panama. The French had failed twenty years earlier. But under Roosevelt, the nation was under the assumption that failure was not possible.

But it was more than current events and national sentiment that led Thomas to be skeptical of the accolades being showered on Horatio Jackson. History was full of examples of the fleeting nature of praise and glory. And though he believed it, he was aware of how susceptible he also was to this need to be admired, respected, and praised by his fellow man. Six years earlier he left St. Mary's because he failed. He failed to effectively control his class and provide a healthy environment in which his students could learn. He failed his fellow Xaverian Brothers, and he failed his God.

The inability to convey his passion for history to the boys under his tutelage was humiliating enough. But having to face the depths of his pride when he tried to hide from his fellow brothers the difficulty he faced caused him to realize that perhaps his heart of service was not as pure as he would have liked.

Late one afternoon after classes had ended, Brother Herman walked into Thomas's classroom, sat in one of the student's seats, and, looking up at Thomas, asked, "Brother Kemp, which battle was the class playacting today?"

Herman's eyes were not dancing the way they did when he shared a humorous story with the brothers. They were fixed on Thomas, unmoving, and grew more accusing as silence filled the classroom. Herman's gaze was stern, his expression echoing the impatient rants Thomas had previously witnessed when Herman disciplined a disruptive student or confronted a boy who was unable to amend his repeated mistakes on the ball field.

"When I am teaching my students," Brother Herman said quietly, "I come to life. I feel invigorated—as if a surge of energy enters my body from somewhere up there." Herman raised his arm upward and pointed toward the ceiling. "There are moments," he continued, "that I almost feel like dancing when I am explaining a theorem or algebraic formula."

Thomas looked at Herman, hoping the confusion he felt would not be interpreted as disrespect. Seconds earlier, he feared the next words that would be spoken, but Herman did not seem angry. He spoke gently, and the description of his joy in teaching almost caused Thomas to break into laughter, or at least smile, as he imagined his fellow brother dancing in his cassock, holding a ruler, instructing the students.

Brother Herman came to life as he taught the students math courses. Thomas was the exact opposite. From the moment he stood before his class, his muscles and limbs tightened, and within minutes he felt drained, uncertain how he could survive the remainder of the day.

With this realization, he approached the prefect of the school, Brother Paul, confessed his struggles, and discussed options. They came to the arrangement that Thomas would temporarily leave St. Mary's, attend St. Bonaventure College in mid-state New York to study instrumental music education, then return to St. Mary's with the intent of leading the boys to pursue their musical talents.

Yes, music was a passion for Thomas. His mother sat with him at the piano in their home from his earliest memories. His ability to play music at parties and get-togethers throughout the years brought joy to those who listened. But if he failed to inspire his students while teaching history, could he not also fail in leading them in their study of music? This was the foremost fear in Thomas's thoughts as the train started for Baltimore. And if he failed at music instruction, what next? Would the brothers send him away to study baseball? Come back to the school and give the boys lessons to improve their fundamentals on the field?

The boys loved baseball. So much so that the most effective mode of punishment was to not allow the disobedient, disruptive child to participate in that day's baseball competition. The corporal punishment common in many of the other institutions was rarely wielded at St. Mary's. And this punishment was a blow for the brothers as well, for most of them held even a greater passion for the game than did the boys. The opportunity to teach and train the children in fundamentals, then watch them compete against one another, was a welcome diversion from the usual monologue-type instruction they practiced throughout the day.

When baseball was the topic of discussion, when the word was even mentioned, Thomas stopped whatever he was saying or thinking or doing and waited, hoping to hear something that would bring to memory an experience from his childhood or add to his reservoir of knowledge. When he joined the brothers and they learned of his baseball acumen, they immediately introduced him to Brother Herman and Brother Mathias.

"Your father played for a mining team near Cincinnati?" Brother Herman asked during their first meeting.

Thomas recalled being surprised by the question.

"The Redlegs?" Brother Mathias asked with raised voice.

Thomas remembered smiling, raising his hand, and shaking his head. "My father never played ball. Never approved of my playing."

And then Thomas narrated for the two brothers his story—his play on the lots and fields of Cincinnati. While still an early teen, he was invited onto rosters of the various trade teams surrounding the city. On Monday he could play for the dairy farmers, on Thursday for the railroads, and on the weekend for the blacksmiths. After one Saturday of playing two doubleheaders, he was approached by a no-nonsense sportswriter interested as to why a young teen was playing with grown men. Thomas's skills improved, but he was never the best on the diamond. His play never rose to the level where he was offered money for his services. Yet this sportswriter treated him special. He took him to eat at restaurants and cafés after ball games, invited him over to his home for supper, walked with him in the park, all the time talking baseball. The writer could have spoken to others, but others avoided him—he didn't drink, he didn't stay out late into the nights. Thomas assumed that because of this oddity, the writer was forced to write his articles based on the observations of a teenager who lived as clean a life as he himself. And this was how his friendship with Ban Johnson had begun.

"Through the years," Thomas had explained to the two brothers, "we have stayed in touch. Since he became head of the Western League, I don't hear from him as often. But on occasion I receive a telegram inviting me to a game."

"Ban Johnson?" Herman repeated. "You are friends with Ban Johnson?"

Though the question was asked in a tone of awe more than of disbelief, Thomas felt he needed to add more details of his interactions with someone of Johnson's renown. "Well, it's not that he sends me tickets so I can get in the game for free. I'm in the seats to work."

"To work?" Brother Mathias asked.

"I study the tendencies of the players, record them, analyze them, write a report for Mr. Johnson. He passes the information to his coaches and players, and they try to use it for their benefit in future ball games."

Brother Mathias raised his arms, then clapped his hands, then wrapped his arms around Thomas, embracing him, swaying him back and forth. "Do you know what this means?" he shouted at Brother Herman, his voice crescendoing through the school's halls. "We've got another coach for the boys!"

Brother Mathias was a gentle giant, the tallest, broadest man Thomas had ever met. His skills on the ball field gained the respect of all the boys at St. Mary's. He had no trouble with discipline, for each boy was on his best behavior in Mathias's class so they might earn his favor and garner more of his attention on the ball field. When Mathias wrapped his arms around Thomas, Thomas felt a warmth he hadn't felt since he was a child being praised by his father for the high marks he had earned.

The memories of Mathias, of Herman, the other brothers, and the boys created an intense anticipation. He was conscious of the smile on his face. He wanted to arrive. He wanted to begin the new journey. He wanted do what he had previously failed to do—instill confidence in the boys.

As he looked out the window, watching farms, fields, and towns disappear while the train progressed toward Baltimore, anxiety replaced his optimism. What if he failed again?

A train conductor touched Thomas on the shoulder. "Sir," he said, sounding a bit impatient. "Ticket, please."

Thomas looked up, observing the conductor's irritable expression, realizing he must have been standing at Thomas's side for several seconds.

"Yes . . . sorry . . . sir . . ." Thomas reached inside his pocket and handed the ticket to the conductor.

The conductor punched it. "Going to Baltimore," he muttered. He handed the ticket back to Thomas and walked to the next aisle.

Thomas reached inside his jacket, and as he placed the ticket back in a pocket, he felt the small hardbound devotional he kept with him always—*The Imitation of Christ*—and suddenly realized he had not yet read the day's reading. He held it out before him, lowered his head, closed his eyes, and sat silently before opening to the marked page:

> Some unadvised persons, to gain the grace of
> devotion, have overdone; because they
> attempted more than they were able to
> perform, not weighing the measure of their own
> littleness, but rather following the desire of
> their hearts than the judgement of their reason.
> And because they presumed on greater matters

than was pleasing to God, they therefore
quickly lost His grace. They who had set their
nests in Heaven (Obadiah 4) were made
helpless and vile outcasts; to the end that being
humbled and made poor, they might learn not
to fly with their own wings, but to trust under
My wings (Psalm 91:4).

"Amen," Thomas whispered, feeling shame that he agreed with the words of Thomas à Kempis but was unable to abide by them. He looked out the window again. More farms, more fields, more towns. The closer the train traveled to Baltimore, the more poignant his stabs of anxiety, not only that he may fail again in the classroom, but fail because he would choose to trust in his own efforts more than he could trust in his God.

Had not God shown his faithfulness? Thomas asked himself.

To this question, Thomas inwardly shouted, "Yes!"

Yes, he had, in many and varied ways. The opportunity to study at St. Bonaventure under great musical geniuses, to earn his degree in music education. Encountering on campus two of the nation's greatest ballplayers—John McGraw and Hughie Jennings—while they took college courses during the off-season, engaging them in classroom discussion, and assisting with drills for the Bonaventure ball club. Being invited by Jennings to follow him to Cornell and assist with the college club there, and as

Jennings studied law, Thomas worked in churches and schools, directing choral groups, gaining confidence in his ability. All the while, the brothers graciously extended his time away, ensuring him that his return was anticipated and welcome.

Life was full of the good—the graces and kindnesses of the people in Thomas's life, his family, his friends. But it was also full of the bad—the death of an elder brother, the grief it caused his family, particularly his parents. The hurt he observed in the world, the sorrow he observed in the young lives at St. Mary's, and his own failures for which he only could take responsibility.

Turning back to the devotional, Thomas searched for a page with the upper corner folded to mark its location:

Nevertheless, our whole peace in this miserable life consists rather in humble sufferance than in not feeling adversities. Whosoever knows best how to suffer will keep the greatest peace. That man is conqueror of himself, and lord of the world, the friend of Christ, and heir of Heaven.

Whatever awaited him back at St. Mary's, success or failure, Thomas knew his future was in the hands of his Creator. He knew that blessings and sufferings would fill the days and months and years of his life, and he knew that his Companion would never leave him or forsake him.

He took a deep breath, then released a satisfying sigh. He tilted his head toward the window, rested it on the seat's head cushion, watched the passing farms and fields and towns, and fell asleep.

* * *

The train pulled into Union Station several minutes before four in the afternoon. Thomas exited, swung the strap of his suitcase over his shoulder, and ran toward the trolley depot. He boarded the Charles Street trolley heading south toward Lombard Street, and once it arrived at the intersection of Charles and Lombard, he jumped onto the street, walked four blocks west, and waited for the arrival of the next trolley on the Wilkins Avenue line.

Once he found a seat, his car jolted forward, waking him to the realization that he had not once thought of Alexander's orphan child the entire day. In fairness, Thomas had thought of the child daily over the past six years, feeling regret and shame that his decision to leave St. Mary's and study at St. Bonaventure was made just several days after the child was handed to him by Alexander. Thomas knew the child was being cared for, that he was perhaps in the best facility for a child in his circumstances. But nonetheless, he felt some responsibility for leaving St. Mary's since he was the one who convinced the other brothers and administration to allow the child to be raised within the walls of the school.

He did not know what the child looked like. Over the past six years, when he sent and received telegrams from Herman and Mathias and inquired of the boy, their response was always, "Fine. William is doing well."

He was completing his classwork satisfactorily. The letters Mathias and Herman wrote over the years filled in a bit more detail, but not much. He did not know the color of William's hair or whether his skin was light, olive, or dark. He remembered holding the infant six years earlier and attempting to determine the child's nationality, imagining from what country his parents originated.

The trolley entered the southern section of Federal Heights, and in the distance Thomas spotted the towers of St. Mary's rising above the fields and surrounding homes. Several minutes later the school's white picket fence came into view. He heard the distant sound of a wooden bat smashing a leather ball and the increased level of cheering.

Even before the trolley made its stop, Thomas could distinguish the tall figure at the sidelines. Garbed in his robe, holding a bat in his right hand and a ball in his left, Brother Mathias tossed a ball up, and with a gentle upward swing of the bat, the ball sailed toward a group of boys waiting about two hundred feet away.

Thomas smiled. He was home.

Chapter 2

Thomas raced to the front entrance, opened the door, and dropped his luggage on the floor. Bending to his knees, he unlatched a side pocket of his suitcase and removed his mitt.

Each field was busy, filled with boys of all ages. In the field closest to the buildings of St. Mary's, two dormitories of the youngest boys were playing against one another. In the field just to the left, older boys were being led in fielding drills by Brother Mathias. In the farthest fields, the oldest boys had been split into their four dormitories, with one game being officiated by Brother Herman and the other by Brother Paul.

Thomas shut his eyes and took a long breath, embracing the aroma of the thick fields of green. The late winter rains had caused catastrophic flooding in the Ohio, Missouri, and Mississippi valleys, but the East Coast had reaped the benefits of the heavy rainfall, with fields that surpassed the colors of any spring in Thomas's memory and promised bountiful harvests. The ball fields of St. Mary's had absorbed the rainfall well.

A constant chorus of chatter mingled with the intermittent sounds of batted balls and the muffled thump of caught balls. A tide of increased chatter ebbed and flowed from each field in response to the events occurring amongst each dormitory.

He heard children cheering from one of the furthest fields as a base runner slid in safely at the plate. In the other game of the older boys, the defense had just turned a double play that Thomas described to himself as acrobatic and charming. The boys on the field with Brother Mathias were all smiling, chasing the soaring fly balls, trying to prove their worth by making the next successful catch. What Thomas found most curious was that the boys were not pushing and shoving one another, trying with all their effort, regardless as to sportsmanship, to make the catch—an occurrence that regularly required swift discipline. But there was none of this. The boy closest to each fly ball would lift his arm, calling, "Mine," or "I've got it!" The others gave way to their classmate fortunate enough to be closest to the path of the ball hit by Mathias.

Thomas sat on a bench just to the left of the third-base dugout of one of the younger dormitory teams. Usually, these boys' skills were lacking and their hunger to learn was keen. Thomas leaned forward, resting his arms on his knees, witnessing the genuine joy on each face. During his previous tenure, he remembered the faces of children frowning on the ball field, frustrated and overwhelmed by an error committed that proved costly to the team. But these incidents were quickly forgotten as long as the boy could experience a moment of heroism in the not-too-distant future. The trouble was when the skill set of a child would not allow him to ever experience a heroic moment. But none of the children in the field were wearing a sad countenance. He studied each face closely and saw only the looks of heightened concentration, intensity, and eager anticipation. The shortstop had just made a diving play to his left and made a strong throw to first base, the ball beating the runner. He raised one finger toward the other infielders, then turned toward the outfielders, still holding his one finger in the air.

"One out," he shouted.

All the boys in the infield were clapping their hands into their mitts, yelling words of encouragement to their pitcher. A brother Thomas did not recognize was shouting instructions to the infield, motioning the second baseman to move further toward the first baseman and for the shortstop to move close to the second base bag. Another brother signaled instructions to the outfield, motioning them in similar arrangements as the infield. The center fielder appeared to be the only one to see the instructions, and as he moved to his left, he leaped in the air wildly, getting the right fielder's attention. With exaggerated motion, he lowered his arms and simultaneously made a looping motion across his body, stopping them near his left hip—the hand gesture, Thomas recognized, for the word *move* in sign language. Immediately afterward, the boy joined his hands together and spread them apart quickly, as though forming a straight line. The right fielder nodded, turned to his left, and raced closer to the right field foul line.

Curiously, no words were spoken by either of the two boys. Thomas concluded that the brothers had successfully integrated the hearing-impaired children into the same games as the others.

The batter hit the next pitch sharply toward the right field line, but it was chased down by the right fielder who, after making the running catch, lifted his right hand to his lips and swiped his hand in gratitude toward his teammate. He mouthed the words, "Thank you," and the boys smiled at one another.

To his left, the group of boys shagging fly balls raced toward the left center field area of the outfield, congregating as though they were awaiting some momentous event. Several minutes earlier the boys were on best behavior, displaying sportsmanship not normally observed among preadolescents, but now the boys were cautiously pushing one another, using hips and arms and legs to create an area they could call their own on the grass field.

Brother Mathias appeared to be waiting for the commotion amongst the boys to end. When it did, he tossed up a ball with his left hand and hit the ball with the bat in his right. It sailed in the direction of the congregated boys, but far past them, so that only those in the back of the group had a chance to chase down the ball and catch it. Whereas before, Mathias would wait for a ball to be thrown back to him before he hit the next fly, now he tossed another ball from his left hand before one of the boys had even caught the first ball.

Thomas saw the first ball be caught by a pudgy kid who ran faster than his body should allow. He raced down the ball, caught it, turned, and with a strong throw from his left arm got the ball to Mathias in one bounce, directly on target, allowing Mathias to catch it with his left hand and immediately toss it in the air and hit another fly. If one of the balls was not returned close enough for Mathias to retrieve, he pulled another ball from a bag resting on a chair next to him.

This rhythm continued. At times, three fly balls were in the air simultaneously, Mathias appearing as a circus clown, juggling a ball and a bat, popping up fly balls. The boys chased them across the thick grass of St. Mary's, giggling, cheering one another, and anticipating that the next ball hit would be theirs to claim. Mathias was targeting all sections of the outfield, allowing different boys the opportunity to catch up to one of the balls.

After five minutes, most of the boys looked exhausted. Thomas saw many bent over, hands resting on their knees. Others were falling on the grass, lying with their faces toward the sky, their chests grasping for more air. And a few, wearing that eager expression, were hoping still for another chance at glory. But Mathias dropped his right arm to his side, still holding the bat, and with a broad sweep of his left arm and a high-pitched whistle, waved the boys toward him.

The boys raced toward Mathias and within seconds picked up the balls strewn over the infield and walked toward the buildings of St. Mary's. The group of about twenty, with Mathias in the center, was just several yards away when Mathias looked toward Thomas. His eyes widened.

"Brother Thomas Kemp!" he proclaimed, gently making his way through the group of boys, then spreading his arms and embracing his friend.

"Boys," Mathias directed, "say your greetings to Brother Thomas."

A chorus of "Hello" and "Good afternoon" and "Welcome to St. Mary's" was shouted by the group.

Turning back to the boys, Mathias held his right arm out, holding the bat and pointing it directly at Thomas, and said, "Brother Thomas is a baseball genius, boys! Not only is he a confidant of the president of the American League, but he has studied with, tutored, and befriended John McGraw and Hughie Jennings!"

The boys' faces transformed. Just seconds earlier, they had greeted Thomas with cordiality. Now, their eyes were fixed on him with a look of awe and eagerness, as if they expected to hear an insight that could increase their skills.

"And," Mathias continued, "he is our new music teacher."

At this piece of information, the boys looked at one another, then at Mathias, then at Thomas, scratching their heads and not speaking.

Mathias laughed and instructed the boys to return to their dormitory and clean up for supper.

As the boys departed, Mathias turned to Thomas. "You made good time. We weren't sure if you'd arrive today."

"Scranton Station was in chaos. Everyone was heading east to witness the Winton entering New York. Freed up all the other routes. The trains south were running ahead of schedule."

"That's all the boys were talking about this morning. We couldn't get them to concentrate in class. Brother Paul was receiving updates by telegraph and relaying them to each room so we could post the progress on the board. We tried to integrate it into our lessons. Herman constructed a lesson around the calculation of mileage and velocity. I reviewed the progress of transportation—Pony Express and the railroads. Science classes were trying to figure out how the automobile engine operates."

"They made it?" Thomas asked.

"They did," Mathias answered.

Seeing Mathias, witnessing the camaraderie he had with the boys and the joy he saw on their faces as they interacted with him, had almost caused tears to form in his eyes.

"We've got a surprise for you," Mathias announced.

"For me?"

Mathias turned toward the front entrance. "Follow me!"

The halls were filled with the sounds of hundreds of boys upstairs preparing for supper—shouting, running, jumping, laughing. These sounds had haunted Thomas six years earlier, but now, the chaos felt welcoming.

"This way." Mathias pointed toward a classroom in the far opposite corner of the building. He stopped and held out his hand, motioning to the doorknob. "Open it," he invited.

Thomas reached for the knob and turned it. Stepping inside, the first thing he noticed was the arrangement of chairs—not in rows, like the other rooms, but in three concentric semicircles. And in front of each chair was a stand holding sheets of music.

Thomas turned his head and looked at Mathias. Mathias motioned toward the back of the classroom. "There's more."

In the far left corner were stacks of boxes.

Mathias began laughing as he slapped Thomas on the back. "Open one of them!"

Thomas reached for the top box on one pile and removed the tape around it. Inside was an assortment of smaller boxes, all sealed. He reached inside and opened one box.

His heart stopped a moment when he reached inside, feeling the cold, fragile metal of a clarinet's silver keys. He raised the midsection of the instrument into the air, admiring its shining black body. The next box also held a clarinet. He opened one of the other larger boxes, discovering it contained flutes.

There were also oboes, bassoons, saxophones, trumpets, trombones, and in the two largest boxes, two tubas.

It was the end of July, yet Thomas felt as though he had just experienced the wonder of a Christmas morning.

* * *

Later that evening, after the boys finished supper and Thomas had been escorted through the three dormitories and introduced to the boys, he returned to the classroom where he had left his luggage. He opened his satchel and took out a folder that held his favorite sheet music.

He reentered the main hall, turned left, and walked toward the chapel. Herman mentioned in a recent letter that an organ had been donated four years earlier by a wealthy family in Baltimore, and that ever since Brother Adrian had transferred to Lexington, it had not been used. Thomas was anxious to feel the cool touch of the keys, press them cautiously, and discover whether the organ's entrails were working properly.

When he opened the chapel doors, he was surprised to see two of the boys sitting in the second-to-last pew on the far left side of the chapel. Each had his head down, with a book resting on one knee and a pad of paper on the empty pew beside him. They appeared to be studying, and neither boy showed any signs of noticing his arrival. He stopped while still holding the door, unsure if he should proceed, not wanting to disrupt them. He shut the door with as much care as possible, unsure whether he should test the organ.

Still, even with the door creating a subtle *thud*, the boys did not budge or turn their heads to see who had entered.

Though there was sufficient light for the boys to study, the chapel lamps were dim compared to the main hall, and it took Thomas several moments before his eyes adjusted well enough to search for the location of the organ. Fortunately, it was on the far right end of the chapel, opposite the boys studying in the pews.

As he walked toward the organ, he glanced to his left, considering whether he should ask the boys if his playing would be disruptive. Immediately, he recognized them both. They were the two outfielders from the game Thomas watched earlier on the Little Field—the center fielder and the right fielder who signed to one another during the game. The center fielder must have caught Thomas in his peripheral vision, for he looked up and at first looked fearful, but after Thomas smiled and waved his hand in greeting, the center fielder smiled and waved in return. Then he looked back down at his book and wrote some notes on the sheet of paper next to him on the pew.

Assured that his organ playing would not disrupt two deaf children, even if his skills were rusty, even if the organ's pipes were rusty, he proceeded to take the covering from the organ, place the music on the rack in front of him, pump each pedal several times, then cautiously, hopefully, stroke middle C. No sound.

Thomas closed his eyes and sighed. He held his breath and tapped it again.

A faint *ehh* emerged from the console.

Again he pressed the key, and this time a confident bellow echoed through the chapel.

He glanced at the boys. Neither one stirred.

Thomas ran his fingers up and down the keys, completing the C major scale, followed by the other majors, then the minors.

The boys still were immersed in their studies.

Taking a deep breath and closing his eyes, Thomas let his memory rush through the eventful day: the coach to Scranton, the train from Scranton to Baltimore, the trolley to St. Mary's, watching the boys on the Big Field and the Little Field, opening the boxes in his new classroom.

He opened his eyes, scanned the notes before him, and his fingers danced across the keys, his soul shouting the words:

> All creatures of our God and King,
>
> Lift up your voice and with us sing
>
> Alleluia, Alleluia!
>
> Thou burning sun with golden beam,
>
> Thou silver moon with softer gleam,
>
> O praise Him, O praise Him,
>
> Alleluia, Alleluia, Alleluia!
>
> Thou rushing wind that art so strong,
>
> Ye clouds that sail in heaven along,
>
> O praise Him, Alleluia!
>
> Thou rising morn, in praise rejoice,
>
> Ye lights of evening find a voice,
>
> O praise Him, O praise Him!
>
> Alleluia, Alleluia, Alleluia!

And all ye men of tender heart,

Forgiving others, take your part,

O sing ye, Alleluia!

Ye who long pain and sorrow bear,

Praise God and on Him cast your care,

O praise Him, O praise Him,

Alleluia, Alleluia, Alleluia!

Thomas finished with his eyes shut, surprised at his ability to recollect the notes. His fears of the organ's health were unfounded, and the last notes still echoed through the chapel as he again looked toward the two boys in the second-to-last pew.

No longer were they studying books. They were in passionate dialogue, arms and hands expressing to one another things that created large grins, laughter, and exaggerated nods of agreement and disagreement. Based on Thomas's limited recollection of American Sign Language, it appeared they were discussing or studying or arguing about one of their class assignments. Whatever it was, they seemed to be enjoying it.

It was clear that his organ playing had not disrupted their studies. So he pulled out another sheet of music and began playing the tune of "Amazing Grace."

When he was nearing the end, he looked toward the back pew and noticed the center fielder was alone. The boy sat with his legs folded on the pew, looking at Thomas, his lips pressed as if he were trying to determine a complex math problem.

As Thomas gathered the sheet music from the rack and began to walk toward the chapel doors, he heard a voice mumbling.

"One plus one is two. Two plus two is four."

Thomas turned toward the boy.

"Three plus three is six. Four plus four is eight. Five plus five is ten."

Now directly across from him, Thomas walked closer, to the center of the aisle.

"Six plus six is twelve. Seven plus seven is fourteen," the center fielder continued.

Feeling as though he were prying, Thomas turned to leave.

"Hello," the boy said, his eyes again showing some trepidation as if he committed some infraction for which he might be reprimanded.

Thomas raised his hand, as he had minutes earlier when he thought the child was deaf.

"You're much better than the other organ player," the boy said softly.

Thomas cleared his throat and walked closer to the boy. "You study here often?"

The boy nodded. "Yes, sir. Timmy and I come in most every night."

"Timmy is your friend. The right fielder?"

The boy laughed. "Yes, sir. He and I did not finish the notes on the board this afternoon. We had to rush to the Little Field to make sure we were chosen for the game."

"I see."

"And sometimes," the boy continued, "the custodian erases the notes at night. If we don't get there before him, they might be gone."

"And Timmy is deaf?" Thomas asked, trying to deduce what the center fielder's story might be, why a hearing boy would be studying with a deaf child.

"Yes, sir," he answered.

"And you are not?" Thomas cringed after he had asked it.

"No, sir."

The boy looked down and began arranging his books and papers.

Thomas looked at the books the boy was placing in his bag. "*A Primer for American Sign Language?*" Thomas read.

The boy stopped packing his bag and looked up.

"There was a list of French kings on the board," he began. "Timmy and I were trying to memorize them. I use it to help me figure out how to say things."

Then the boy looked away from Thomas, placed his hands in his pocket, and got a faraway look in his eyes. "You know what Brother Phillip told us today?" he asked. "France had a king all the way back to 509. That's almost fifteen hundred years! Then, all of a sudden, in 1792 they don't want a king anymore, so they chop off his head."

Thomas studied the boy. He seemed to be puzzling over something a boy his age ought not to puzzle over.

"May I sit?" Thomas asked.

"Yes, sir." The child straightened his posture, pushed his bag of books and paper aside, slid next to Thomas on the pew, and raised his knees to his chest.

"How old are you?" Thomas asked.

"Six years and one month, sir."

"You don't need to call me sir. My name is Thomas. Brother Thomas."

The child smiled and nodded. "Yes, sir."

"And what is your name?"

"William, sir. But the other boys call me Kid or Willy."

"Very well. Rest assured, William, that one day you will understand why the French no longer wanted a king. You will learn, if you continue to listen in class, read, and seek answers, why the line of kings ended, and you will learn that something horrible and something wonderful happened to bring the line of kings to an end. You will learn that a new ruler arose who changed the course of history. And rest assured that I will be happy to listen to any more questions that may arise during your days at St. Mary's."

* * *

It was the best of days, it was the worst of days.

During breakfast, just after Thomas had taken his first sip of coffee in the dining commons, he saw Brother Herman rush toward him and place a telegram next to his plate of eggs and bacon.

"It must have come last night," Brother Herman speculated, "after we were all asleep. Was at the front door, next to the milk."

Thomas opened it and immediately recognized it had been sent from his old friend in Cincinnati, now the president of the newly formed American League. He read:

BOSTON MASSACHUSETTS, 1010P SEP 7, 1903

BROTHER THOMAS KEMP

ST. MARY'S INDUSTRIAL SCHOOL FOR BOYS, BALTIMORE

PILGRIMS RUNNING AWAY WITH THE PENNANT <STOP>

WOULD LIKE TO UTILIZE YOUR SERVICES <STOP>

IF OTHER BROTHERS CAN SURVIVE WITHOUT YOU <STOP>

TRAVEL BETWEEN BOSTON AND NL CITY <STOP>

LIKELY TO BE PITTSBURGH <STOP>

BEGINS OCTOBER 1 IN BOSTON <STOP>

I WILL SEND TWO TICKETS FOR EACH CONTEST <STOP>

COULD BECOME TRADITION <STOP>

BAN JOHNSON

Thomas followed Brother Herman to the telegraph room. Brothers Paul and Mathias were waiting with eager smiles. From their expressions, they must have known the nature of the telegram and were eager to learn of its specific message.

"He's requesting that I attend all the games," Thomas revealed.

"And?" Herman asked.

"It will likely begin on October 1—in Boston."

"And?" Mathias asked.

"He's sending two tickets for each game."

Mathias and Herman smiled, eyes widening.

Brother Paul quickly dashed any illusions they might have had. "Thomas," he said cordially, "you will go. Take as long as you need. The boys can survive two weeks without music instruction."

Then Brother Paul turned to Mathias and Herman. "No other brother will be attending the games. We can't deliberately have more than one of us away during fall schedule."

Herman and Mathias grimaced, but they nodded.

Brother Paul continued. "Thomas, you can find a friend of yours outside these walls that will be eager to attend?"

"I will."

Thomas sat at the telegraph and wired his reply to Mr. Johnson.

That same afternoon, Thomas again was beckoned to the telegraph office. Only Brother Paul was awaiting his arrival.

"Sit, Thomas."

Thomas sat in the chair opposite the seat from which the messages were typed. Brother Paul turned that chair and faced Thomas.

"We received confirmation from the school in Beverly," Brother Paul announced. "Timmy has been accepted for admission."

For several months, since his return to St. Mary's at the end of July, Thomas had gradually gained an intimate knowledge of the changing philosophy surrounding the education of the hearing impaired throughout the country. It explained why there were now so few deaf children at St. Mary's—in fact, Timmy was the only deaf child in the school since Thomas had returned. During his previous tenure, there had always been a handful of deaf children.

Timmy and William were inseparable, always speaking with their hands, laughing, eating meals together, playing on the same team on the Little Field.

Now, as the nation was growing more convinced that the best way to integrate a deaf child into communities was by teaching them to read lips and speak audibly, the use of signing was gradually becoming viewed as a hindrance to progress. Teaching sign language was discouraged, and the brothers were getting pressure from those inside and outside the church to join in the movement toward oralism. As a result, whenever a hearing-impaired child came to St. Mary's, they would attempt to transfer the child to one of the leading schools for deaf children. They regularly reached out to schools in Massachusetts—one in Northampton and one in Beverly. Normally, within recent years, the deaf children would only reside at St. Mary's for several months, but Timmy had been there his whole life, and the longer he stayed, the more difficult the brothers feared the transition would be for him.

Brother Thomas learned that Timmy had arrived several months following William's arrival. Both boys matured at normal rates, learned to walk and eat and go to school along with the other boys their age. But because the stay of the other deaf children never lasted longer than several months, Timmy was unable to build any meaningful friendships—except with William.

Brother Mathias had recognized the boys' special bond and with the approval of the other brothers had purchased signing primers for both boys and arranged for a signing tutor to visit St. Mary's each weeknight for two years. William became Timmy's best friend and interpreter.

Mathias, Herman, Paul, and Thomas were all skeptical that the transfer of Timmy to the school in Beverly would serve his best interest. His application was completed, signed, and mailed by Brother Paul, with the understanding that the oral method would offer Timmy a better chance of integration, but the brothers were hoping his admission would be denied because of the immense grief it would bring both Timmy and William.

Brother Paul's words echoed though the room. "Timmy has been accepted for admission."

Thomas lowered his head, knowing that the next step in this horrible chain of events was his responsibility: breaking the news to William.

As he stood, a thought entered his head, something that could possibly lessen the blow for at least one of the boys. A crazy idea, one that Brother Paul certainly would not approve.

"I was wondering," Thomas began, looking hopefully at Brother Paul, "whether perhaps I could take Timmy on the train to Beverly."

"Of course," Paul said. "I will arrange it."

Thomas noted Brother Paul's quick response and added, "And could William accompany us?"

Brother Paul looked at Thomas skeptically, as if he knew he was not finished. He did not answer, and his expression of curiosity evolved into accusation.

"Since we will be near Boston," Thomas proceeded, "William can use the other ticket I will be receiving from President Johnson. We will travel from Boston to . . . well, wherever, Pittsburgh likely . . . back to Boston, and then back home. We'll be gone, say, for two weeks."

Chapter 3

Although Brother Thomas had spoken to the boys, and though the conversation took place in Brother Paul's office with both Brother Paul and Brother Mathias present, the finality of the news did not appear to affect Timmy and William the way Thomas and the other brothers had feared it might. Even now, the boys sat opposite each other on the northbound train, paying close attention to the passing scenery, signing to one another whenever either of them saw an unfamiliar object or event outside. Thomas felt invisible and didn't mind. The boys were immersed in the excitement of venturing outside of St. Mary's. Still, he feared the pending doom when the boys recognized the finality of their separation.

Thomas imagined the trauma over and over. He would be holding William's hand, leading him away from the doors of the school in which Timmy would now be raised. Would William begin to cry? Would he refuse to leave the school's premises?

It was strange, but it seemed both boys showed only excitement, as if they were fully aware of the long-run benefits for Timmy. Perhaps their anticipation for the train adventure distracted them from contemplating what life would be like without one another.

As the train passed through New Jersey, the tall buildings of New York City could be seen in the distance, like a toy city made of blocks. Thomas studied the boys, not wanting to miss their expressions when they first caught sight of the skyline. Timmy was the first to notice the large city. He turned to William and tapped him on the shoulder, then, extending his hand in the city's direction, pointed at it.

"Is that New York?" William asked Thomas.

Thomas smiled. "It is."

William turned to face Timmy. He held out both hands, turning his left palm upward and making a first with his right hand, extended his right pinky and thumb, then slid his right hand back and forth across his left palm.

He turned back toward Thomas. "I thought we'd pass through it—I told Timmy we would. But he didn't believe me. It's so big!"

William turned again toward Timmy, pointed at his face, then extended his arms while shrugging his shoulders. Thomas was fairly certain William was reminding Timmy that he had previously told him that they would see the city.

"Are we getting off here?" William asked.

"The train will stop to drop off passengers and get new passengers, but we will be staying on the train."

William frowned, looked at the city, and when he turned back toward Thomas, William's frown had grown more severe. His eyes were fixed on Thomas with an accusing stare, as if he had been betrayed.

William crossed his arms, looked out the window, then turned back to glare with the same expression.

Thomas shook his head. "Not today, William. Not enough time. We need to get there by tonight. If we get off, that will not be possible."

Twenty minutes later, the train pulled into Grand Central. Most of the passengers exited, leaving all but several seats empty. The boys seemed to have run out of discoveries, for they were no longer signing to one another. Both sat in their seats, feet dangling over the edge and brushing the train's carpeted floor. Occasionally, William looked at Thomas. He was biting his lip and tilting his head toward the exit door each time a new passenger entered. He leaned his body to the left toward the aisle and began to move his left leg, as if testing Thomas's resolve. But when Thomas moved his head ever so slightly to the left and to the right, William reluctantly moved his left leg away from the aisle, fixing his eyes back on Thomas, his stare intensifying.

As the train left Grand Central, Timmy tried to engage William in a conversation, but William would not respond. He waved his hand and did not acknowledge his friend. Within minutes, Timmy fell asleep.

William seemed to be empowered by rage. His glare was making Thomas uncomfortable, afraid that he was about to release the anger he had bottled over his short six-and-a-half years, thus creating an ugly scene in their compartment. At first Thomas had found William's disappointment amusing, the look on his face sweet and charming. He had not seen William react this way at the school and assumed that in all the books he had seen William read, somewhere he had garnered a fascination with New York. To be this close and not be able to explore must be the cause of the ugly expressions.

Thomas sighed and glanced back at William to see if his stare had grown more condemning. But William was asleep. His head was resting on Timmy's shoulder, his arms still folded across his chest. Several minutes later, Thomas fell asleep also.

When he awoke, the first thing he noticed was that both boys were awake. They were sitting still, engaged in no dialogue, not looking out the windows, not studying the passengers, their eyes focused on nothing in particular. Eventually, Timmy grinned at Thomas as if greeting him with a "Good morning." William no longer appeared upset, but something else was clearly disturbing him, and Thomas was fairly confident he knew what it was.

It seemed both boys realized that soon their separation would occur. The reality of the purpose of the trip was manifesting itself. The train arrived in Boston around five o'clock, then continued north to Beverly. They arrived at the depot around 7:30 and walked one mile east to the school. Thomas carried a large suitcase in his right hand, holding his clothes and some of William's. He also strapped a large duffel bag across his shoulder, which held Timmy's belongings. Each boy carried a small satchel that held a few articles of clothing.

The boys sat on a bench outside the administrative office as Thomas spoke to a receptionist. Minutes later, an instructor walked down a long hall and approached the bench on which the boys sat. He signed his welcome to Timmy, bending to his knees and extending his hand. Timmy stood, frowned, and lowered his eyes. He shook the instructor's hand and looked back up, turning to Thomas, his eyes filled with pleading and desperation.

Thomas handed Timmy's duffel bag to the instructor and placed his hand on William's back, gently prodding him forward. The boys embraced and simultaneously looked to the floor, then raised their hands to their eyes. As if they read each other's mind, each extended his right hand, placing it atop the other's head as though blessing one another.

The instructor led Timmy down a long hallway.

About thirty seconds later, they turned right and disappeared.

* * *

Brother Thomas and William walked back to the depot and arrived just in time to catch the last southbound train for Boston.

They arrived in the city after ten, and Thomas paid a coach to take them to the Buckminster Hotel where Ban Johnson had made their reservations.

By the time they arrived, William had fallen asleep, so Thomas carried him upstairs, took off his shoes, and placed him under the covers of one of the beds before returning to the coach and retrieving their luggage.

On the other bed, the bed in which Thomas would sleep, atop the pillows was a leather satchel with a golden buckle. Atop the satchel was a note:

Wednesday, September 30, 1903

Welcome, Thomas,

Look forward to seeing you tomorrow morning—I will fill you in on the details over breakfast. As I am sure you are aware, you will be working for me and the Pilgrims.

Inside this satchel you will find the rosters for both teams. Please try to study the Pittsburgh roster as much as you can prior to our meeting, paying careful attention to Wagner, Clarke, and Phillippe—we must not allow those three to beat us. Based upon your previous work, I have also enclosed the materials you will need.

Do not be alarmed. I know you have not done this for several years, but after discussing our need for more in-depth analysis with Hughie Jennings, he suggested hiring a Xaverian Brother he came to know at St. Bonaventure and Cornell—you can imagine my surprise and enthusiasm!

The letter infused Thomas with energy. Minutes earlier he had felt drained, but now he feared his excitement might keep him awake. William was sleeping peacefully. As Thomas looked down at him, he knew sleep was what he also needed if he were to be of any value to the Boston team. So he stuffed the letter into his pocket, washed his face in the basin, placed the satchel at the foot of the nightstand, and, without removing the covers from the bed, laid his head on the pillow. He turned his head to find the sweet spot, wiggling his body and head until he felt just right.

Before he shut his eyes, he noticed the satchel, even in the dark. Somehow the gold buckle was shiny enough to catch his attention. Inside of it was the information he needed to study in hopes of formulating a strategy for BJ and the Pilgrims.

"Help me wake in two to three hours," he whispered.

Sighing, he closed his eyes, thinking of the satchel, the Pilgrims, and the Pirates.

Thinking of Timmy. Thinking of William.

Thomas awoke while it was dark.

William was sleeping soundly in the bed closest to the window.

For an hour, Thomas studied Pittsburgh's roster, focusing on the strengths of their key players. His eyes strained, struggling to read the reports in the weak light emanating from the lamp on the nightstand. He felt confident he could formulate a strategy for how the Boston pitchers needed to pitch to Wagner and Clarke. But the Pirates ace pitcher, Deacon Phillippe, was another matter. Studying the notes compiled by the American League office did not help. There was no clear way that Thomas could suggest for the Boston hitters to approach their plate appearances against him. His arsenal of pitches and ability to control where he threw the ball were so precise that a hitter's best chance was to wait for one of his rare mistakes. It was no wonder, Thomas concluded, that the papers were heavily favoring the Pirates to win the series.

He placed the report into the satchel and went to the washroom. He deliberated over whether he should continue wearing the Xaverian cassock or change into his street clothes. Technically, as long as he was William's escort, he was representing the brothers—therefore, wearing the cassock was proper. But he wondered whether his holy attire at the ball games would attract unwanted attention. To remain undisturbed at the games was crucial. He looked at William, then at the clothes Thomas had pressed before they left St. Mary's, organized neatly on the chair next to William's bed. He envied William for the lack of effort he would have in deciding what to wear. Thomas had set out the clothes on the chair just like his father used to do when he was William's age. The finely pressed knickers rested on the chair's seat. Each stocking was draped over an arm of the chair. The shirt was folded and halved, hanging atop the backrest, and the light coat was hooked over one side of the chair's backrest, a golf cap hooked over the other.

He walked to the closet and unhooked the cassock. BJ's response would be key. When they met for breakfast, he would look for a reaction that implied BJ's approval or dislike, and if necessary, he'd come back upstairs to change. Otherwise, he'd see how the fans reacted and reevaluate tomorrow.

He straightened his collar and woke William. "Breakfast," he announced while lightly shaking William.

William sat up and looked toward the room's window. The sun was bright and the air had a hint of dryness.

As William rubbed his eyes, Thomas said, "A fine Indian summer."

William did not seem to care about the weather, for he usually asked for clarification with regard to a topic he had likely never heard discussed. Instead, he jumped from the bed, smiling, and began to dress.

Thomas led William down the stairs and toward the hotel's café. BJ had left instructions in the satchel to meet him there at seven o'clock. He hoped

William would not be frightened by his friend. He knew William had heard of Ban Johnson, but it seemed to Thomas that William was not yet old enough to recognize the privilege of meeting a person of such prestige. As they approached the booth in which he was sitting, BJ was reading the *Boston Globe*. And this was a good thing. It meant BJ was wearing his spectacles, and the way the glasses rested on his face created a schoolboy persona that made him look less intimidating. He was wearing an expensive suit, a bright red silk tie, and a tweed vest. He stood as the two approached. As large a man as Thomas remembered him to be from the last time they met five years earlier, he seemed to have grown even wider.

"Welcome, Thomas!" he exclaimed.

Thomas extended his hand. BJ grabbed it and shook it vigorously then embraced him.

Thomas placed his hand gently on William's back and prodded him forward. "William," he said, "this is Mr. Johnson."

William stepped forward and smiled. "Thank you for the ticket, sir."

BJ laughed as he stooped downward. "You are very welcome, young man. You are one of Brother Thomas's students at school?"

"Yes, sir."

"You are a ballplayer?"

William shrugged. "I like playing."

"Well, William, have you ever been to a professional game?"

"No, sir."

BJ clapped his hands, then raised them over his head as he straightened his posture. "Excellent! Excellent!" He laughed in a deep tone, with such force that he coughed immediately after.

BJ cleared his throat when his coughing ended. "And you like pancakes, William?"

"Yes, sir."

"Then sit, and they will bring them shortly. Brother Thomas and I need to talk some business."

BJ handed a thick envelope to Thomas. "It's one hundred dollars. Ten dollars for each game. It's best of nine, so I rounded up."

"That's very generous—"

BJ interrupted. "Tickets for each game are inside. You're close to home, always opposite of Pittsburgh, at an angle. I want you to study their signs, see if they have any tendencies, mannerisms, anything we can use to our advantage."

Thomas reached inside the satchel and took out some notes he had made earlier in the morning. "This is what I've come up with on Wagner and Clarke. But I'm curious—you're not worried about Leach or Sebring?"

BJ held out his hand. "Limited resources. Limited time. Anything on Phillippe?"

"I got nothing."

BJ laughed. "None of us have. He's an enigma, that one. Nobody can figure him. Lucky for us that the other two are out of commission—or almost. Leever hurt his shoulder a few days ago in a shooting accident. We may see him, but word is that his pain is severe, not much chance he can be effective if they decide to use him. And Doheny had another episode and they've checked him into a hospital, so he won't be available. Phillippe is it!"

Thomas nodded. This was good news indeed. Still, they would have to overcome Phillippe if they were to win the series.

BJ cleared his throat. "I know you, Thomas. I know what you're thinking. Don't sell yourself short. I didn't ask you here to be nice and give you a hundred bucks and free tickets to each game because I like you. You've got the sense. You can discover things others can't. Just sit in those seats, study Phillippe. Look for anything that may assist us, and you're going to have a lot of opportunities to study him. Without Leever and Doheny, they're left with Phillippe, and it's likely he'll pitch most of the games."

* * *

BJ rushed out once he gave the instructions, leaving the morning paper next to his breakfast dish. The front page was dominated by stories and pictures of the players from each team. Thomas reached for it.

The *Globe*'s headline read, "READY TO BATTLE FOR THE WORLD'S CHAMPIONSHIP." Underneath, the subheading read, "The Approach of the Pirate Crew. Today They Assault the Citadel."

Below the headlines, a cartoon portrayed the Pittsburgh team, not in their grayish-blue uniforms but as a disgruntled, unruly mob wearing overgrown beards, bandanas, and eye patches. They brandished sabers and guns and knives, holding high their flag as they stormed the capitol building. Protecting the inhabitants of Boston from this attack, perched on the edge of the cliff that overlooked the storming mob, was the Boston team, armed with their wooden bats and classic literature of baseball stratagem. At the center of Boston's defense was their manager, Jimmy Collins, and Cy Young, Boston's veteran ace pitcher.

A scraggly-looking member of the Pirates team sat with his musket and saber, his eyes focused away from the action as if he were speaking to the reader. From his mouth, a dialogue bubble contained his warning: "Dis is fer cuttin' into old Cy."

Just behind him, his teammate Honus Wagner, with his knife between his teeth and his gun pointed toward Boston's manager, yelled, "I will make me dose ten home runs alretty yet."

Cy Young replied to Wagner's threat, looking down upon him with pity. "You mean 'nein,' don't you, Hans?"

Thomas softly chuckled and looked at William, who seemed interested in what caused his laughter. "You enjoying your breakfast, William?"

He looked at Thomas and nodded exuberantly, his cheeks puffed and straining to contain the pancake he was chewing. On his plate, fragments of the cakes rested in pools of syrup. Thomas figured he still had several minutes to study the paper until William would require some other sort of entertainment.

Next to the cartoon of Pittsburgh storming the city, the lineups of both teams were listed. The names Phillippe and Wagner and Clarke were all there. In their midst was the name Leach, and near the bottom of the lineup, playing right field, was Sebring. Although BJ did not seem concerned about the potential threat of these two Pirates, Thomas felt each would play some role in Pittsburgh's fight.

He glanced at William, who was still enjoying his meal, turning his head left and right, watching the movement of people through the hotel's lobby. Thomas reached inside the satchel, taking out a few sheets of paper. He pulled a pen from his shirt pocket and wrote on top of one of the pages, in bold print, "DEACON PHILLIPPE." Just below the name, at the center of the page, he wrote "Outside," then underlined it twice. He turned the sheet of paper over and wrote "Inside," and placed double lines beneath it also. He drew a straight line from the underline to the bottom of the page, creating a large "T". He turned the page over again and drew another straight line from the word "Outside" to the bottom. He took a deep breath, closed his eyes, and began:

<u>*Outside*</u>

6 foot, 180 lbs

Right hander

Fastball: B+

Curveball: B+

Control: A+

Mixes pitches well

On the other side of the dividing line, he wrote:

<u>*Outside*</u>

Durable

Lefties have slightly better success

No obvious weakness with form

All pitches good — guessing pointless

Swing at any pitch in zone to liking since he doesn't miss zone often

He turned the sheet of paper to the other side and wrote:

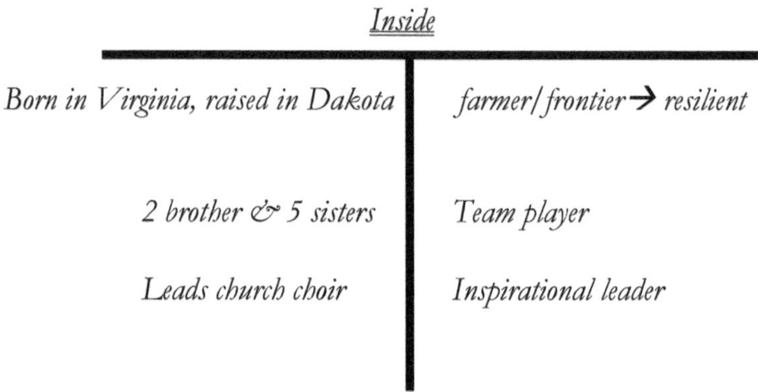

The whole process took Thomas less than ten minutes. Most of the items he had already known about the Pirates pitcher, but some he learned earlier that morning when reading through the reports BJ placed inside the satchel. Thomas did not feel it was sufficient information to construct a strategy for the Pilgrims to implement. Nonetheless, it was all they had, and it was Thomas's responsibility to find weaknesses. At this point, the only hope was in the growing reality that Phillippe would be pitching in several of the games. The longer the series extended, Thomas surmised, not only would it provide him with more of an opportunity to discover Phillippe's liabilities, but it would surely add fatigue to the throwing arm of the Pirates ace.

Thomas placed the report back into the satchel and looked across the table. William's eyes focused beyond Thomas, darting to the left, then the right, concentrating, it seemed, on whichever hotel guest earned his attention most. When his eyes could not keep pace with the activity, he turned his head, then his body, pushing himself away from the table, perhaps to get a more panoramic view.

And then, the fidgeting stopped.

His eyes fixed.

Thomas turned slightly to follow William's stare. At the hotel's front desk, a well-dressed man was speaking with a hotel employee. The man appeared to be paying his bill and showed no signs of being exceptional in any regard, nothing that Thomas imagined could capture a six-year-old's attention. Behind him was a young woman holding the hand of a boy about the same age as William. The man finished his business with the hotel employee, placed a document in his jacket pocket, smiled at the woman behind him, wrapping his arm gently around her shoulder, and kissed her on the check. Then he gently took her hand in his. As they walked toward the hotel's exit, the young boy skipped between them, unlocked their hands, grabbed his father's right hand and his mother's left hand, and used their strength to leverage himself as he raised his feet from the ground, swinging between them.

Thomas studied William. His eyes were following the young family until they left the lobby and could no longer be seen.

"You enjoyed the pancakes?" Thomas asked again, hoping to distract William from whatever dark thoughts were dancing in his mind.

William did not answer.

Less than twenty-four hours earlier, when their train was fueling at New York's Grand Central Station, Thomas had read an anger in William that he had previously never seen. Later that evening, he saw a deep sadness when William and Timmy were separated. Now, the boy's face seemed vacant as the young family left the hotel.

Thomas had yet to tell William about the agenda for the day, hoping to keep it a surprise until the last possible moment, wanting to hold that card until he was desperate.

"William," Thomas said with a hint of excitement.

William looked up.

"Yesterday when we were at the train station and stayed on the train . . . do you remember?"

William nodded and frowned.

"You wanted to see a big city? Walk in a big city?"

"Yes," William said softly.

"Do you know where we are this morning? What city we are in?"

William shrugged. "Boston?"

"Some may disagree with me, William," Thomas said as he stood, "but I believe this is our nation's most exhilarating, educated, and history-filled city."

Thomas extended his hand, motioning William to stand.

"And I will be your guide."

* * *

The game was scheduled to begin at three. It was a few minutes after eight. Plenty of time to explore. Once they left the hotel, they headed west until they reached the Cotton Ridge Bridge. As they were crossing to the north side of the Charles River, William stopped, raced to the western railing, and pointed at a squadron of swift-moving vessels quickly approaching. He turned, looking to Thomas. "What are they?"

The distant voices of the Harvard crew were chanting their rowing pace. The bright crimson jerseys of each eight-man shell created an awe that even Thomas felt. He was grateful for the timing of their crossing, enabling William to witness the morning workout. Once the shells passed underneath, William skipped to the other side, bent to his knees, and poked his head past the bridge's rails, watching the shells glide past. He turned to Thomas, looking up, smiling, as if he wanted to say something and couldn't find the words.

Once they reached the end of the bridge, they turned left onto Charles River Road until they entered Harvard's campus. Thomas led William past the buildings, not wanting to linger long. From Harvard, they walked east to Bunker Hill Monument, south to the port at which the USS *Constitution* rested, then to visit the Old North Church and home of Paul Revere. Finally, they made the long walk west, back toward Huntington Avenue Grounds. Thomas reached in his pocket and opened his watch. It was one o'clock. The game would begin in two hours.

Cy Young took the mound, grooming the rubber with his right leg, kicking dirt from its edge. As he began his warm-up tosses, the chorus from thousands of fans was incessant and loud. Occasionally, Thomas could make sense of one or two of the conversations near him, but for the most part, the noise was incomprehensible, like thousands of cicadas fiddling on a muggy summer evening. He was studying his notes, looking up occasionally to study Phillippe as he threw to his catcher, Eddie Phelps, on the sidelines next to the visiting dugout. Thomas frowned, not confident he would find anything of use for BJ or the Pilgrims.

He felt like a child at times, looking in awe at Honus Wagner, amazed that he was sitting so close to the greatest player in the game. He felt guilty for writing a report and handing it to BJ that morning—a report that could undermine the man he most admired. He was curious as to whether his suggestions would be utilized, curious whether they would be successful.

Wagner was mesmerizing even as he stood in front of the Pirates dugout, throwing softly to third baseman, Tommy Leach. His hands were huge—almost as if they were drawn by a cartoonist. They didn't seem to belong on a body his size. As for his ears, they too suggested his creator to be a political cartoonist and appeared to belong to a baby elephant. Though he was muscular, he was not tall. He was stalky and a bit pudgy. Still, he was quick, his reflexes unmatched on the field, and the strength of his arm was unparalleled. Thomas shook his head in disbelief at the greatness of Wagner, disbelief that a grown man, a teacher of youth, a Xaverian Brother, was gaping over a man younger than himself simply because of his skills on the ball field.

He looked down at William sitting quietly to his left, on the edge of his seat, legs in constant motion, head turning toward the loudest noise whether it be on the field or amongst the spectators. He had yet to ask any questions even though Thomas had made it clear he could ask as many as he wanted. Before they entered the gates, Thomas lowered to his knees, struggling to keep his balance, his cassock making the task difficult and awkward. "Any time," he said slowly, looking directly at William, "whenever you have a question, anything you are wondering, ask me. Even if I look busy or deep in thought. You understand?"

William had nodded, yet an hour later he still had asked nothing.

Just after they had entered through the gates off Huntington Avenue, the most prominent feature directly before them was the billboard announcing the sale of Dr. Swett's root beer, with white print on a bold black background. Thomas needed no prodding from William. He immediately approached the sales vendor and asked for two cups. He handed the vendor ten cents, then quickly reached inside his pocket, searching for another ten-cent piece. When the vendor returned with the two cups, Thomas held up two fingers. "Two more, please."

Thomas bent down to William. "Hold out your hands, William," he instructed.

William obeyed.

While keeping a light grip on each cup, making sure William had a secure hold, he placed them into William's hands. "William," he declared, "this will be our nourishment. No sips, no tasting, until we reach our seats. Understand?"

William nodded. His eyes widened as he gazed into the dark, bubbling concoction.

Forty minutes had passed since William finished his first cup of soda. He showed no interest yet in the second. All the activity in the stands, on the field, and the anticipation of the game seemed to keep William preoccupied. Even Thomas was struck by the expanse of the field. They were seated just to the right of home plate and had a panoramic view, not only of the field, but also of the city beyond. The offensive smells outside the walls of Huntington could not dampen the spirits of the fans. On their way to the front gate, Thomas and William had passed a pickle factory, a brewery, a bean cannery, stables, and a chemical factory. The aroma of each was unpleasant enough, but their mixture in the air of the stadium was indescribable.

Their seats were located just as BJ had promised—at an angle and distance that enabled Thomas to observe the activity inside the Pirates dugout. He considered his fortune to be at the game, to have seats in such a prime location, and to receive the tickets for free. Beyond the right field fence, fans not so fortunate had stormed the field, overcome the police, and climbed atop the outfield fence, content to watch the game while straddling the top.

Seated beside Thomas were a banker and his wife. Thomas had exchanged greetings with them as he and William arrived, but he hoped they would not be talkative neighbors, disrupting him from his responsibilities. The wife of the banker was one of the few women in the stands, and her red Victorian touring hat stood out amongst the sea of black fedoras. They were a curious couple, Thomas thought, imagining the husband to have a normally austere, businesslike demeanor at work, but here, he and his wife, though dressed in proper upper-class attire, were standing to cheer and scream. They sang along with the Royal Rooters, a band playing popular tunes, now playing the fan favorite, "Tessie":

> Tessie, you make me feel so badly;
>> Why don't you turn around.
> Tessie, you know I love you madly;
>> Babe, my heart weighs about a pound.
> Don't blame me if I ever doubt you,
>> You know, I wouldn't live without you;
> Tessie, you are the only, only, only

William was standing but showed no signs of enthusiasm or comradery with the crowd. He wasn't swaying along with the band's tune like those near him. In fact, he stood still, hands in pockets, face sober.

"Is everything all right, William?" Thomas asked.

William smiled. "Yes, Mr. Tom," he answered, then turned his attention back toward the circus around him.

Thomas looked at William curiously. He had always addressed Thomas as "sir," never anything else. Now, out of the blue, in the midst of the chaos, he addresses him as "Mr. Tom," as if the adventures they shared over the past two days had created the necessary familiarity to allow such a transition.

He placed his papers in the satchel under his seat. He stood with the rest of the crowd, and though he did not sing, he clapped in rhythm with the band. William was not pleased with this—he lightly hit Thomas in the side, shaking his head and frowning even more severely than on the train the previous evening. He pushed his hands deeper into his pockets.

When the band stopped, the last notes of the trumpets' blasts echoed off the grandstands. The home plate umpire placed his mask over his face, pointed his index finger at Cy Young, and shouted, "Play ball!"

The crowd hushed.

Ginger Beaumont, the Pirates center fielder, hit Young's first pitch well. But his direct counterpart, Chick Stahl, caught it easily for the first out. The next batter, Fred Clarke, hit a weak foul ball behind home plate that was chased down by the catcher, Lou Criger.

In less than two minutes, Cy Young had disposed of the first two Pirates hitters. The Boston fans were standing, applauding, shouting so loudly that William raised his shoulders to just under his ears, unwilling, it seemed, to remove his hands from his pockets and use them to shield from the crowd's uproar. His frown had grown and he was biting his lip, leaning forward.

Tommy Leach, the Pirates fine-fielding third baseman, was up. Cy had put him in the hole with two quick strikes. The uproar in the stands grew louder. Thomas looked down at William. It almost seemed he was squinting now, too scared to watch.

And then it happened.

Leach laced Young's next pitch down the right field line, the ball screaming over the head of Boston's first baseman, Candy LaChance, and past the right fielder, Buck Freeman, into the crowd of fans behind the roped-off outfield boundary. It was a ground-ruled triple per the arrangement of both teams before the series began.

Leach stood at third. William's eyes were now open—no squinting. Biting his lip, still leaning forward, still frowning, he stood on his tiptoes.

Next up was Wagner. Young's first pitch was a looping curve on the outside of the plate. The Pirates shortstop slowly reached his bat out to contact it and hit it just hard enough for a lazy fly safely into left field. Leach scored. Wagner at first. William took his hands out of his pockets.

As soon as Young made his first pitch to Kitty Bransfield, Wagner ran for second, well ahead of Criger's throw. Wagner was now at second. William punched his fist in the air and said softly, "Yes!"

Although Cy fooled Bransfield on the next pitch so that he grounded the ball weakly toward second, Hobe Ferris, a normally sure-handed fielder, muffed it. Bransfield was at first, Wagner at third. William was smiling.

On the first pitch to Claude Ritchey, Bransfield broke for second and Criger threw the ball too high, over the heads of the infielders, into center field. Wagner scored. Bransfield ran to third. The Pirates led 2–0. William clapped his hands lightly twice, then looked at the fans around him. They did not seem to notice. Most were wearing somber frowns. Some men were removing their hats and scratching their heads.

Young ended up walking Ritchey. Once again, with men at first and third, the Pirates attempted a double steal, but this time Criger bluffed his throw to second, then quickly turned and threw to third, hoping to catch Bransfield by surprise. But Bransfield was ready and slid safely back into third as his teammate arrived safely at second. With Bransfield at third base and Ritchey at second, Jimmy Sebring, the Pirates right fielder, hit a clean line drive into left field, scoring both his teammates.

The Pirates had just scored four runs, with two outs and nobody on base. William was jumping now, clapping, smiling, and screaming, "More. More."

Phelps, the Pirates catcher, struck out. And the top of the first was over.

The banker tapped Thomas on the shoulder as the Royal Rooters began to play "Tessie." "You two from Pittsburgh?" he asked.

"No, sir," Thomas answered. "Baltimore."

The banker leaned forward, getting a closer look at William. "What's his story?" the banker asked.

"Wagner fan," Thomas answered, unconvinced that was all there was to William's excitement.

"No doubt," the banker said, shaking his head and plopping back into his seat.

"He's so cute," the banker's wife added.

Thomas turned again to study William, who apparently heard the exchange and was sticking out his tongue toward the couple.

Deacon Phillippe jogged to the mound, picked up the ball on the back side of the rubber, and tossed his first warm-up pitch. His stoic expression reflected no consciousness of his team's offensive explosion. He made quick work of Patsy Dougherty, striking out the Pilgrims leadoff hitter. Jimmy Collins fell next, also striking out. Chick Stahl hit a clean single to left, but it happened so quickly that Thomas had no chance to observe if there was a weakness in Phillippe's arsenal that perhaps Stahl had discovered. The next batter hit a lazy fly to right, and the inning was over.

Though Pittsburgh had an uneventful top of the second, Phillippe struck out the next three Boston hitters in the bottom of the inning. As he trotted back to the Pirates dugout, the Boston fans stood and applauded—not in their normal raucous banter, being led by the Royal Rooter band, but with a healthy, genuine acknowledgment that a fine performance was being given by the opposing pitcher. Surprised by this response, Thomas smiled and turned to observe the spectators around him.

William tapped him on the shoulder. "What's this?" he asked, raising his hands toward the adoring crowd, shrugging his shoulders, and looking a bit confused.

"Baseball," Thomas answered. "True fans of the game."

The Huntington crowd had little else to celebrate. Isolated Pirates' runs in the third and fourth innings put the Pilgrims in a large deficit. The chasm grew wider in the seventh when Sebring hit a line drive past Boston's right fielder and raced home for the game's only home run. The Pilgrims finally got to Phillippe in the bottom of the inning, scoring two runs and adding another in the bottom of the ninth, but it fell far short, ending the game with Pittsburgh on top by the score of 7–3.

"You enjoyed the game?" Thomas asked William on their way back to the hotel. It wasn't that he really needed to ask the question, but William still had given no verbal commentary of his experience, had asked no questions about strategy, had not even asked Thomas about what he was doing during the game as he shuffled papers and wrote.

When they entered their room at the Buckminster, William ran to the bed and sat on its edge, swinging his feet and bouncing on the mattress.

"I'm curious, William," Thomas said. He shut their room's door, placed his satchel next to the nightstand, then walked toward William. "Why the

Pirates? How or when or why did you become a Pittsburgh fan? Is it Wagner?"

Immediately, William frowned, leaped from his bed, reached into his back pocket, and laid out on the table near the room's window the morning paper BJ had left at their breakfast table. He flattened the paper, running his hand over the front-page cartoon of the Pirates storming the shores of Boston.

"Look at them!" William hissed. "Sitting up there so sure of themselves with those grins and smiles. It makes me so angry. It's like they think the Pirates haven't got a chance."

He was pointing at the line of Boston players atop the cliffs of the city as they watched the Pirates racing across the beach. As he pointed, his frown grew deeper, and as he looked at the players portrayed in the cartoon, his eyes narrowed. He took a deep breath, turned away from the paper, and looked up at Thomas. "That's why."

"William, you know why they call the people at the game 'fans'?" Thomas asked.

"No, sir." William's frown lessened and his eyes widened.

"It is a shortened word, William, for a much longer word."

William's eyes widened more. "Really?"

"Fanatic."

"What's it mean?"

"Come here." Thomas led William toward the room's mirror and faced him toward it.

"There—you're looking at one. One game and it's clear to me. It was clear to that couple sitting next to us. It was clear to everyone at Huntington Park today that William Jennings is a baseball fanatic!"

As Thomas made this statement, William smiled, then giggled. He skipped back toward his bed, then began to bounce up and down on the edge.

"Why do you hate the Pirates?" he asked. "Why are you making all those notes to help the Pilgrims beat them?"

Thomas felt his heart buckle. He couldn't help but grin. He sat in the room's only chair and faced William. "You knew what I was doing?"

William did not respond. But after several moments he seemed to understand it was a question and nodded.

"The man we met this morning is paying me to find something that will help the American League team beat the National League team."

"Why?" William asked.

"Well, because BJ, my friend, is the president of the American League."

William did not appear to understand. "President? Like Teddy Roosevelt?"

"Well, sort of. I guess. Maybe . . . yes, okay . . . yes . . . like Roosevelt."

"How?"

"Well, Mr. Roosevelt is paid to defend our country from other countries—to help us succeed in the world. He does this by helping our businesses succeed or by helping our schools flourish, or by building the navy. And BJ is searching for ways to help his teams—the teams in the American League—do better than the teams in the National League."

"Can I help?" William asked, walking toward the satchel at Thomas's bedside.

Thomas looked at William peering down at the satchel and felt something foreign, a type of kinship and a mixture of pride and affection. He wondered if perhaps this is how a father feels toward his child, wondering if he ought to reconsider the vows he made years earlier.

"And what about the Pirates?" Thomas asked. "You wouldn't mind assisting me, even if it meant the Pirates could lose?"

William turned to face Thomas. He looked deep in thought. "How many games will they play?"

"Well," Thomas answered, "it's a best-of-nine series. Whoever wins five games first is the champion. So at least five, at most nine."

William began counting on his fingers. "So," he continued, "we want the Pilgrims to win at least four games? Yes?"

Thomas felt he understood William's logic: in order for the maximum number of games to be played, each team would have to win four games.

And if William was a true fanatic, the number of games to experience was of more importance than his team winning the championship.

"I suppose that is correct," Thomas answered.

"Then," William continued, "I will help you win four games."

* * *

The next morning Thomas woke William at eight o'clock, rushed down for a quick breakfast, and headed east to Boylston Avenue.

Before laying his head down to sleep the night before, Thomas had glanced at the newspaper William placed on the table. Next to the story of the championship's opening game was the anticipated arrival of England's Honourable Artillery Company into Boston Harbor on Friday, October 2. Upon their arrival they would be welcomed by Boston dignitaries and invited to march into the heart of the city. Thomas guessed such an event would involve marching bands and hoped to witness the events to learn techniques he could teach his students. While William was still sleeping, he rushed down to the main lobby and purchased the morning edition of the *Boston Globe*. On the front page was a map of the parade's route.

It would begin at the harbor just after ten, move west toward the capitol, and then meander to Beacon Street, hugging the north end of Boston Commons. Eventually it would turn left onto Arlington, then left on Boylston and would move along the south end of the Commons. Thomas planned to intercept the parade at the intersection of Arlington and Boylston, at the far southwest corner of the park.

Thomas had heard of the highly regarded Salem Cadet Band that would be welcoming the British visitors. He wanted to arrive at Arlington and Boylston before they passed. They were the first to emerge around the corner of Beacon Street. At first the only sound they made was the drum corps lightly tapping their sticks against the metal of their instruments, matching the cadence of the forty-piece band as they marched along the western perimeter of the park.

"I can't see," William said, stepping as high as he could onto his toes.

Thomas picked him up and placed him on his shoulders as the first notes of "The Star-Spangled Banner" were played. Thomas felt his heart pounding, felt his skin prickle, and he too stepped high onto his toes. The members of the cadet band were in their teens. Most were not much older than the boys in his music classes at St. Mary's, yet the sounds emerging from their instruments were crisp, clean, hearty, and heart-stirring. The quality of their play was equivalent, Thomas thought, to the college bands at St. Bonaventure and Cornell.

While the cadets passed Thomas and William, turning onto Boylston, they began playing "God Save the King." As though on cue, the first regiment of the Honourables turned onto Arlington. They were dressed sharply in bright red jackets and deep blue trousers with a narrow red stripe down the seams. They wore round dark blue caps adorned with stripes of red braid. Behind them came the National Lancers dressed in bright red coats and white helmets, playing vignettes from various European march sequences along with excerpts from "Yankee Doodle" and "Dixie." Behind them, another regiment from the Honourables arrived, wearing slightly different blue-and-red uniforms.

All around, the crowds were cheering and singing loudly along with the tunes. They were raising hands, waving flags from both countries, and jumping in rhythm with the music. People had opened windows on the upper stories of buildings along the southern perimeter of Boylston and were waving flags, shouting, and singing.

Within twenty minutes the procession passed, but the spectacle of the adoring crowds followed in their wake as the parade headed back toward the capitol. Thomas glanced at his pocket watch and realized the game would start in less than two hours. He grabbed William's hand and led him back west toward Huntington Grounds.

"That's the second time," he heard William mutter.

Thomas looked down toward William. "What's that? Second time?"

William pointed toward the back end of the last regiment, barely visible from where they stood. "Yesterday. And today."

Thomas stopped, bent down, and looked at William inquisitively. "What happened yesterday and today?" he asked.

"The people," William answered. "They cheered for the other team yesterday, just after Phillippe struck out five of the first six batters. Now they cheer for the country we fought in war."

Thomas narrowed his eyes, uncertain whether this was childhood curiosity or an indication that William was pondering some philosophical dilemma beyond his years.

"When's the game begin?" William asked, apparently oblivious to the confusion he had just caused Thomas.

Thomas reached again inside his pocket. "Hour and a half. Better hurry."

By the time they arrived at their seats, the Boston players had taken the field and the first pitch was moments from being thrown by Bill Dinneen. Thomas removed his papers and pencil from the satchel and set it under his seat. William had initially been full of energy on their walk back toward Huntington, skipping and whistling the tunes from the parade, but the closer they got to the stadium, the more quiet he had become. And once he sat in his seat, William hunched his shoulders, lowered his eyes, and whimpered, "I wish Timmy was here."

Thomas did not want to hear this. He had work to do. He wanted to ignore the implications of William muttering these words. He felt guilty for wanting to ignore them. After Dinneen had struck out Beaumont on a called third strike, he looked back down at William, who was curled into a ball on the seat, his head resting on the seat's metal railing. He didn't wake until the game ended.

He hadn't missed much. The Pirates were silenced. Dinneen had only given up three singles and struck out eleven Pirates. The most exciting moments were when Boston's leadoff hitter, Patsy Dougherty, hit a leadoff inside-the-park home run. The cheering crowd caused William to stir and adjust his sleeping position, but it did not fully wake him. When Dougherty hit a second home run in the sixth, this time the ball bounced off the top of the left field fence, then proceeded into the street. But not even the crescendoed cheer as the ball bounded out of the stadium was able to wake William.

After the game, on their walk back to the hotel, William asked Thomas about the agenda for the next day. "Will there be another parade in the morning?"

"You're not too tired to wake early?"

"No, Sir Thomas!" William skipped ahead, turned, and with eyes wide asked, "What time?"

During the game while William was sleeping, Thomas overheard several conversations regarding the visiting British delegation. He learned they would spend most of the day in Providence, Rhode Island, but there would be another short marching event beginning at Faneuil Hall in the morning before the send-off from South Station.

"We'd need to wake at seven," Thomas said. "There is another parade, much shorter and further from the hotel. It will begin around nine. You think you can wake up? Ready for another day of long walks?"

The next morning Thomas woke, surprised to see William standing at his bedside, his face several inches from his own.

They made it to Faneuil Hall just in time to hear the Salem Cadet Band begin "The Star-Spangled Banner." William was clasping his hands together, smiling and glancing at Thomas as if he wanted to share his excitement. His body was swaying with the deep rhythm of the bass trombones and tubas. When the crisp melody from the trumpets emerged, William unclasped his hands and clapped along with the rest of the crowd.

The cadet band played the same songs in the same order as they had one day earlier, and the British band also followed the same program as the day before. But William's enthusiasm and wonder seemed to grow with each note. And as the British visitors moved out of Faneuil toward South Station, William followed in their wake, not even waiting to ask for Thomas's permission.

William shouted whatever those around him were shouting. "Good, good! Very good! You're all right. Long live the king!"

Through the streets, draped from windows and doors were American flags, English flags, and red, white, and blue buntings. Thomas would not have thought it possible, but the noise and raucous admiration with which the Bostonians welcomed the British visitors was even greater than on the previous day.

By 10:30, the British Honourables had boarded their train and left for Rhode Island. By twelve o'clock, Thomas and William arrived at Huntington Grounds. Already, three hours before starting time, a larger crowd than had attended the previous two games was flooding the streets outside the stadium. Thomas sensed an agitation amongst the crowd and, wanting to avoid any confrontation, walked past the stadium, hoping to find a quiet place to eat before returning.

But in each street there were crowds. At first Thomas turned down one street or alley that appeared to be an escape, but each turn eventually led him to a larger crowd. As the minutes passed, the crowd grew larger and louder. Thomas heard several recurring conversations as he and William struggled to stay together. He grasped William's hand, instructing him to stay close.

"There are no tickets available!" Thomas heard fans yelling. "They're sold out!"

He heard others shouting, "They are going to sell more standing room so we can watch on the field . . . "

Then later, "No, all those tickets have already been sold."

Thomas reached into the pocket of his cassock, searching for his watch. It was now 2:15. He and William could barely walk, the crowd was so thick. He wasn't even sure he knew what street they were on and was uncertain how to reach the gate they entered for the previous two games.

Suddenly, a rush of men leaped upon the wall, scaled it, and entered the stadium. More followed in their wake, and soon a rush of others followed, recognizing that this may be their only opportunity to watch the game.

"Sir Thomas!" William shouted.

Thomas saw William pointing toward the wall. Just several feet from them, two young boys not much older than William were climbing the fence, their legs being tugged by two boys likely in their late teens or early twenties. The two older boys, in their efforts to make it over the wall and onto the field, had torn the pants and shirts of the younger fans.

Immediately, Thomas rushed to the older boys and pulled them off the wall and onto the ground. At first the two fans looked upset, but upon seeing Thomas, their eyes moving from the bottom of his cassock to the top of his collar, they looked down toward the ground and ran several yards further to find a suitable path over the wall.

The two younger fans had fallen to the ground, failing to make it to the other side. They stood next to William and Thomas and frowned. One of them kicked Thomas in the shin several times, dirtying the bottom of his cassock. The other turned to William and swiped his right fist toward William's face. William's eyes widened, and with a ghastly expression of pending impact, he swiftly pulled his body away from the boy. The boy had swung with such force that, upon missing William's face, his momentum brought him to the ground. He quickly stood, then raced after his friend who had left a shoe imprint on Thomas's cassock.

Thomas was going to ask William if he was all right, but before the words came, he was amused to find a smile growing on William's face.

"That was something," William said amidst laughter.

Thomas reached for William's hand and walked resolutely, searching for their gate. They found it, entered, and rushed to their seats behind home plate.

The mayhem continued. The police were holding fire hoses to keep fans from charging the outfield fence. Just minutes before the game was to start, Ginger Beaumont, the Pirates center fielder, rushed to the right field wall to protect a woman being accosted by the two young men Thomas had pulled off the younger fans on the other side of the fence.

The two umpires had consulted with the managers and amended the ground rules. It appeared that the game would proceed with fans lining the outfield, behind ropes, some even straddling the top of the outfield fence. For the most part, this favored the visiting team. High fly balls that would normally be outs turned out to be ground-rule doubles. And although the Boston team could have benefited from these rules as well, Deacon Phillippe for the most part kept the Pilgrims hitting ground balls or striking out. Thus, when the game ended, Phillippe had won his second game, besting the Pilgrims 4–2.

William was much more boisterous during this third game. After the Pirates took an early 3–0 lead, and whenever Phillippe made easy outs against the Pilgrims, he stood and applauded and shouted, "Good, good! You're all right, you Pirates!"

Though he got several sour looks, most of the fans in their vicinity seemed to share the banker's wife's sentiment of William and allow his cuteness to erase any animosity. Regardless, Boston was down two games to one, and Thomas was no closer to figuring out a way to beat Phillippe.

* * *

On the train to Pittsburgh, William studied the results from the first three games. The past three days he had ripped out the pages from the newspaper and had written down a cumulative summary of each player on a sheet of paper.

"Honus has only two hits," he said, looking up at Thomas with some bitterness. "In nine at-bats," he continued, before Thomas had a chance to respond. "What did you tell BJ about him? Why is he not hitting?"

Thomas raised his head, feeling some pride that William had concluded he was responsible for Wagner's poor showing.

"It was you, right?" William prodded.

"The game is full of chance, William," Thomas began, not sure how to proceed.

"But what did you tell BJ?"

"Tell him?"

"About Honus. How to make sure he doesn't hit well. What kind of pitches to throw him."

Thomas wasn't sure if it was wise to instruct a student in his care about what he was considering.

"Poker," Thomas said. "I suggested they approach Wagner like they would a game of poker."

William's face was blank.

"It's a game," Thomas explained. "A card game."

Still, nothing seemed to register.

"Here," Thomas said as he reached into his satchel for a pack of playing cards. He opened it and began to shuffle the cards. "I will teach you."

William moved to the edge of his seat. "How do you play?"

Within thirty minutes, William was a functional player. Thomas had explained the hierarchy of hands. They wagered the peanuts they had not eaten at that afternoon's game. And they showed one another their cards after each hand in order for Thomas to learn of William's comprehension of the game's finer points.

The woman in the aisle across from them looked crossly at Thomas, eyeing his cassock. She shook her head while making eye contact and muttered "Hmm" several times.

After an hour, William was able to make decisions without having to ask for assistance. And after two hours, he had performed his first bluff.

Thomas had waited for this moment. He wanted to make sure William felt comfortable continuing with this part of the game. After thirty minutes and ten or more bluffs, Thomas felt confident William understood.

Thomas collected the cards and placed them back in the container. "Now, William," he started, "when you keep playing, even when you have a bad assortment of cards, why do you keep playing?"

"Because I want to win."

"But what if I knew you didn't have a good hand?"

"But you didn't know until after I had won."

"So you were guessing I didn't know?"

"Yes! And . . . and . . . guessing you didn't have a better assortment of cards than me!"

Thomas smiled. "So, tell me. William, how can this be similar to a pitcher and a batter?"

Several moments passed and then William smiled.

"You see, William. Wagner has no weakness as a hitter. The only way to beat him is to outguess him. Change the pitch sequence and hope he doesn't outguess you."

"And that's what you told BJ?"

"That's what I told him."

* * *

Game four in Pittsburgh was on Tuesday afternoon. Phillippe pitched again. Phillippe won again. He had given up only one run through eight innings. In the top of the seventh, with Pittsburgh up 2–1, William poked Thomas's side, the first time he had disturbed him during any of the games.

"Yes, William, what is it?"

"Why does he keep his foot away sometimes?"

"Away?" Thomas repeated. "Who? Away from what?"

William extended his arm and pointed at Deacon Phillippe.

Thomas slowly placed his hand over William's extended arm and lowered it, not wanting to draw any attention, regardless of what value William's discovery may bring.

"Tell me," Thomas whispered.

"See? Like now," William said softly, shifting his eyes toward Phillippe. "His right foot—only the back is touching the rubber—yes? See? But not always. Sometimes the whole foot is against it, not just the back."

Thomas nodded, then leaned forward. Phillippe's next pitch was a curveball, crossing the plate for a strike. Again, before the next pitch, Thomas looked closely at Phillippe's right foot, and only the back touched the rubber. Another curveball, this one called a ball by home plate umpire, Hank O'Day. Phillippe received the ball back from his catcher, Eddie Phelps, and looked disappointed—it was a close pitch that didn't go his way. Showing visible disgust with O'Day would be a poor tactic. He nodded and stepped back onto the mound and set his right foot flush against the rubber. He nodded at Phelps's sign and threw a stinging fastball past Boston's first baseman, Candy LaChance. The next pitch was the same—foot flush against the rubber. Fastball.

For the remainder of the seventh inning and through the eighth, Thomas tested the theory: foot flush against the rubber signaled a fastball, foot at an angle meant a curve. Not once did the theory fail.

"William, I am going to ask you to do something for me," he said while he scribbled some instructions on a sheet of paper, folded it, then handed it to William.

"There." He pointed toward a man sitting just above the Pilgrims dugout. "See him?"

"It's BJ," William replied. "You want me to take it to him?"

"Yes, and quickly. Go!"

Thomas had not been this nervous since the day he resumed teaching a few months earlier. He sat on the edge of his seat, tapping his foot, watching William maneuver his way through the crowd. William tapped BJ on the shoulder and handed him the paper. BJ nodded, then placed his hand on the child's head and turned until his eyes met Thomas. They both nodded. BJ opened the sheet, read it, and beckoned the Pilgrims batboy toward the railing, handing him the sheet of paper.

In the top of the ninth, now down by four runs, Boston's player-manager, Jimmy Collins, got a single. Stahl followed his with another base hit. Freeman made it three in a row, scoring Collins and advancing Stahl to third. Parent hit a ground ball to Wagner but beat the throw to first, avoiding the double play and scoring Stahl. Boston was now only down by two. LaChance hit a single and so did Ferris, loading the bases. Farrell pinch-hit for Criger and hit a long sacrifice fly, scoring Parent. Boston was now down one run. O'Brien pinch-hit for Dinneen and popped out to Ritchey, ending the game. Pittsburgh held on for the win and was now leading the series 3–1, but Phillippe had been found out.

Time away from the ballpark in Pittsburgh held adventures of a different sort. The weather was overcast. Thomas would have enjoyed exploring the city, but hiking the hills of "Smoketown" with the risk of being caught in a heavy downpour was not an adventure he thought would excite William. So on Wednesday morning and through the early afternoon, though it did not rain, the two of them stayed in their room at the Monongahela, playing several hands of poker, studying the notes each had been keeping, and admiring the picturesque view from their window overlooking the three rivers and many valleys.

Game five was scoreless through five, each team only getting three singles. But in the top of the sixth, Boston exploded for six runs and followed with another four in the seventh, adding one more in the eighth. They bested the Pirates 11–2 and now trailed the series by one game.

Pittsburgh had pitched Brickyard Kennedy on Wednesday and decided to pitch Sam Leever on Thursday, hoping he had healed from his hunting accident a week earlier. He hadn't—he gave up six runs, and Boston tied the series at three.

Fred Clarke and the Pittsburgh owners begged the Boston organization to delay Friday's game until Saturday, hoping to maximize ticket sales, but Boston refused. Regardless, there was enough rain to convince the umpiring crew to delay the game one day. Though six thousand more fans did attend, Pittsburgh lost 7–3. Phillippe had pitched his fourth game in a week, and it was clear in the first inning that the success Boston had in the final inning several days earlier was not a fluke. They scored twice in the first, twice in the fourth, twice again in the sixth, and once in the eighth. Boston was only one win away from winning the series. Thomas felt confident they would succeed since the final games would be played in Boston.

He had contributed to their success. The Pilgrims had clearly utilized the information he wrote on the note. He had met with BJ prior to the game on Tuesday and fully disclosed that it was William who had discovered Phillippe's tendency. BJ laughed heartily, bent to his knees, and wrapped his arms around the boy. "You are always welcome, young William. The two of you have helped us make it interesting. Let me know if you find any other . . . quirks? Yes?"

William nodded. "Yes, sir."

There were no other discoveries. There were no more wins for Pittsburgh. Down three games to one, Boston won four consecutive games to defeat the Pittsburgh team. The final pitch of the last game was a chest-high fastball thrown by Bill Dinneen to Honus Wagner. Pittsburgh's star player had had a horrible series, having only six hits in twenty-seven tries. Wagner swung at the high strike and missed it entirely. The Boston crowd had been quiet, anticipating the moment. When the ball made contact with Lou Criger's mitt, the crowd roared. Criger tossed the ball into the air, rushed toward his teammates in the center of the field, and celebrated for a few short seconds until the crowd grabbed the players, placed them on their shoulders, and marched them across the field. The Royal Rooter band added to the celebration, blaring "Tessie" as the fans remaining in their seats sang along.

Thomas felt something he could not quite explain. There were tears in his eyes and something like pride mixed with a bit of gratitude that he had the privilege of watching and in some small way participating in the outcome of the games. He looked down at William and watched him clap, shout, and sing the few words of "Tessie" he had gleaned from the eight games they attended. He seemed ambivalent as to who won. He had started as a Pirates fan, but now he was cheering, getting lost in the celebration with the Bostonians around him.

None of this would have been experienced by the boy—none of the joy that Thomas witnessed on his face would have occurred had Timmy not been transferred to the Beverly School for the Deaf, had Thomas not failed at teaching history, had William not been abandoned. Thinking of these things created a stronger surge of tears and more feelings that Thomas could not understand.

Chapter 4

A rhythm emerged during fall semester. Thomas woke at five and walked the school's perimeter, preparing his heart, mind, and soul for the morning devotions he would have upon his return to his room. He assisted the other brothers in waking the boys at six o'clock, then participated in a short homily with the other brothers in the chapel as the boys prepared for breakfast. After the morning meal the boys gathered for a short mass, then proceeded to their classes.

When he arrived in July, Thomas had announced in the dining hall that any boy interested in learning to play an instrument was invited to his classroom for an introductory course in music. The class was scheduled during the first hour following lunch, giving the boys an option to choose one hour of musical training to replace one of the three hours spent in learning a trade. To his surprise, over a hundred boys had attended. After a month of instruction and giving the boys opportunity to try the instruments of their liking, he began testing and assigning the instrument he felt best suited each of them. Upon his return from Boston, he began to sit with the boys individually, listening to their playing and creating a file that separated the boys into three groups—beginner, intermediate, and advanced.

In January, those boys whose names were in Thomas's file proceeded to his classroom after lunch rather than to the three-story workhouse where their classmates trained and worked their craftmanship as cobblers, carpenters, and tailors. The brothers had decided that the boys could practice music for one hour, then return to their assigned craft. Since the time allotted each day for work-related training was three hours, Thomas was able to meet with each of the three levels for one hour each day. The most basic class met for the first hour after lunch, the intermediate met the second hour, and the more skilled musicians met during the final hour.

William, like most of the boys his age, was assigned to the basic class. William, however, learned his scales and fingerings on the trumpet within two weeks. He was able to play any of the basic sheet music that Thomas distributed. By February, Thomas transferred him to the intermediate class. Again, William mastered the reading of different scales and time signatures, so by the beginning of March Thomas moved him into the advanced class.

Thomas was concerned that William would be lost, but again William quickly learned the music. As William progressed from one class to the next, Thomas sat with him individually, as he did with any of the students who progressed to the next level, listening to their playing and determining if their skill had progressed to the point that would enable them to succeed in the more advanced setting. Each time he advanced William, Thomas promoted him reluctantly.

Because of their adventures several months earlier, and because of the unique nature as to how William had come under the care of the brothers,

Thomas was self-conscious to not show favoritism or set a higher standard for William. When he listened to William during their sessions together, there was no denying that he knew the notes, the correct combination of valves to hold, the concepts of octaves and time signature and scales. All that Thomas had taught, William implemented in technique. But the sound that came from the trumpet was anemic. It was flat. It was sharp. There was no life, or art, or beauty. Yet, Thomas advanced boys based on technique, in the hope that with continued practice, the art would follow.

His goal was for each class to have at least ten boys playing each instrument. But the number of boys that could play at a level Thomas considered advanced, or performance-ready, was lacking, so he felt he needed to advance boys based on technique, regardless as to whether the sound emanating from their instrument was clear. With most boys, their playing did improve. With William, it did not.

Several weeks after William transitioned into the advanced group, one of the better trumpeters left St. Mary's. Thomas moved one of the students into the highest chair to replace the student who had left. The remaining trumpeters each moved one seat to their left, and a new trumpeter was added from the intermediate class. William, who had been in the lowest seat before the changes, was now in the second-to-lowest seat. One week later, the newest member of the trumpet section asked Thomas if he could switch seats with William. Thomas asked the boys to remain after class so that he could have each perform for him. The first boy played the scales flawlessly—and with clear tone and pitch. Though William fingered the scales to perfection, when he finished playing he slumped his shoulders and caught his breath. He didn't look up at Thomas to see if his performance salvaged his place but looked down at his shoes, shook his head, and walked to his challenger. Once Thomas instructed the other boy to sit in the chair William had vacated, William sat, head lowered, in the inferior seat.

"Maybe I could try another instrument?" William asked after the other boy left the classroom.

The question surprised Thomas. And it relieved him. "If that is what you'd like," he answered.

William nodded, then once more looked to the floor.

The next day William returned to the basic class and began learning to play the clarinet. Within a month he had mastered the fingerings and could adequately change his mouth's embouchure on the reed to move between octaves. A few weeks later he had learned all there was to learn in the intermediate course. Yet again, the sound emerging from the instrument was painful to hear. But because there were only six clarinet players in the advanced class, he advanced William, hoping once more that with time, the sound would improve.

It didn't.

This pattern continued as William learned to play the trombone, the baritone, and the flute. His capacity to grasp new information surpassed that of any of the other boys, but there was something in his anatomy,

Thomas surmised, that just did not allow him to create an airflow sufficient to play nicely.

One day in mid-June William asked to try the trumpet once more. The advanced band was preparing for a Fourth of July event in which the boys would play "The Star-Spangled Banner." It was near the end of the advanced band's class. They had been rehearsing for the event for the past week, and Thomas was pleased with each boy's improvement. Their sound was clear, crisp, and bold. He could see in each band member a growing sense of confidence and pride in the sound they were creating in unison. And then he glanced at William.

Several notes after the band began, William removed the trumpet from his lips. He rested the bell of the trumpet on his right knee and held the body of the horn by cupping it in his palm, where the valves were located, just as Thomas had trained each boy to do when they had long periods of rest during a piece. But the trumpet players were all playing and William was supposed to be playing along with them. He had closed his eyes. He was smiling. And as his smile grew, so did a peaceful glow Thomas had never seen on the young child's face.

After the hour rehearsal ended and the other boys had left the classroom for their apprenticeship assignments, William was still in his seat, placing the trumpet in its case. He closed the latch and walked with it slowly toward Thomas. He reached his right arm toward Thomas and handed him the case.

"I'd like to begin spending my hour at the tailor shop," he said.

"For all three hours?" Thomas asked, to make sure he understood the boy's intention. "You don't want to play in the band?"

"No, Sir Thomas."

Thomas studied William. He did not look sad. In fact, there were still traces of that peaceful calm on his face that had erased his normal somber and sad expression.

"Besides," William said, "Congo and George say if my work on the second floor keeps improving, Brother Herman may move me up to join them to work on the top floor."

Thomas nodded. He was trying to keep his emotions hidden. He was sad, for his affection for William was far greater than for any of the other children, but he was relieved, for despite all the efforts and intelligence that William displayed, the sound William produced, regardless of the instrument, was a tangible liability for the rest of the band.

The fact that two older boys had taken an interest in William was a good sign. Only the highest-quality shirts were tailored on the third floor—shirts with collars and buttons, shirts that were sold to department stores and created a small revenue stream for the school. The boys with the best vision and hand coordination were the privileged few.

And Thomas knew of the two boys mentioned by William. Congo was the boy the brothers considered to have the most promising future as a pitcher, and George was a baseball genius. Brother Mathias had taken a special interest in him, spending hours perfecting his swing, teaching him to turn his wrists, twist his hips, and make contact with the ball simultaneously. When George hit the ball squarely, which was frequent, it soared higher and traveled further than the best hits of even the oldest boys at St. Mary's. He was an awkward, pudgy child who was about two years older than William. Thomas recalled noticing him that first day he returned to St. Mary's when the young George chased down one of Mathias's long fly balls and threw it back on target with one bounce

On most days, George played catcher, and though he was left-handed, he was still the best of those behind the plate. Somehow, he'd wear the glove on his left hand—his throwing hand—since no catcher's gloves were made for left-handers. He'd catch the ball, flip his left wrist with enough force to lift the ball in the air, then drop his glove while the ball was descending. He'd catch the ball with his now-bare left hand, then throw it back to the pitcher with his left hand. And even when base runners thought this whole process might give them an advantage in stealing bases, once they were thrown out by the pudgy catcher, they'd seldom test him again.

Thomas surmised that William's desire to join Congo and George on the third floor of the tailor shop had something to do with their baseball acumen.

The three hours of apprenticeship and band practice were followed by free time. From 3:30 until supper, the boys had their choice of venturing to the gymnasium, the swimming pool, or one of the baseball fields. An hour of study followed dinner, and then the boys prepared for sleep. By eight o'clock, they were in bed.

William was now seven years old. He and all the boys twelve or younger slept together in one dormitory, while the older boys slept in a separate section of the building. It was a spacious room, warehouse-like, in which over 220 beds were arranged in symmetrical rows and columns. Each bed was draped with white cotton sheets and a single pillow. Next to each bed was a wooden chair. Each night the thirty brothers dispersed amongst the chairs and read uplifting stories of devout characters from the Bible or classic children's literature until that child fell asleep, and then the brother would move to the next chair. The brothers would scatter amongst the 220 beds, their voices not much louder than a whisper, making sure their storytelling would not disturb the brother closest to him.

After thirty minutes, most of the boys were asleep.

Thomas noticed there was one bed the other brothers avoided, or at least left for last. That bed was William's. Most of the children fell asleep within minutes after the brother began to read, but William would not close his eyes until the last word of the story was read—and even then, he would not fall asleep for another ten or more minutes.

The brothers, Thomas learned, were not sure what to do about William. He was not disruptive or rude. Their dilemma was that if he was one of the first children to whom a brother read, he kept that brother from being available to read to another child. Their solution prior to Thomas's arrival was to place him in the bed in the far left corner of the room, and the first brother who read to three other children would then be assigned to read to William for the rest of the evening. When all the other children were asleep, that brother would shut the book he was reading to William and instruct him to shut his eyes. After several months of witnessing the disappointment on William's face when the brother left his bedside without finishing the story, Thomas asked whether it was possible for one brother to spend the whole evening at William's bedside. The other brothers agreed, if Thomas were to volunteer to be that brother. And Thomas volunteered.

He began reading stories from the Old Testament. The boy-prophet, Samuel, was a story that William seemed to enjoy, and he requested it at least once or twice each week. By February, Thomas had read most of the stories from the Old Testament that he felt were appropriate for a seven-year-old child. He even ventured into narratives containing questionable moral behavior. When he read of Tamar and Judah, or Samson and Delilah, or David and Bathsheba, he studied William to see if he understood the sequence of events and nature of sin. He was relieved to see no expression implying a question or shock. He was relieved that William's innocence had not yet been violated.

Near the dormitory door a large box held an assortment of children's books. One evening in mid-March, Thomas grabbed five of them and sat at William's bedside. Whenever Thomas began reading, he first read the title page and the name of the author. If he forgot to do this, William would interrupt and ask about the book's background. After reading the five books, to Thomas's surprise, William was asleep. The next night he grabbed another five, hoping for the same result, but this time William sat up and asked Thomas to read one of the stories from the previous evening.

"Which one?" Thomas asked. "What was it about?"

"The girl who visits her grandmother."

Thomas nodded. "Ahh—*Little Red Riding Hood.*" He searched for several seconds before seeing the red hardcover, placed the other books back into the box, and returned to William's bedside.

Thomas opened the bright crimson cover and began reading. "'A woman had finished her baking, so she asked her daughter to take a fresh galette and a pot of cream to her grandmother who lived in a forest cottage. The girl set off, and on the way she met a *bzou.*'"

William giggled.

Thomas stopped reading. He raised his eyes from the print and waited for the giggles to stop. He realized he had not read the title page, but since he had explained to William the previous evening that nobody actually knew who wrote the original French story, he figured it was not necessary.

"That's funny!" William stopped giggling long enough to exclaim.

"I've just begun," Thomas replied. "The story is anything but funny."

With his right hand, William quickly covered his mouth. "I'm sorry, Sir Thomas. It's the wolf's name—Bzou. It's a funny name!"

"We went over this last night, William. Remember? Bzou is not his name, it is the French word for wolf."

"Yes, Sir Thomas."

And so Thomas continued reading. There were no more interruptions. In fact, once the girl met the bzou in the woods, William leaned his back against the rails, turning his head upward, appearing deep in thought. The sides of his mouth were rising and falling, as if he were solving a puzzle. Before he had a chance to ask, William's head slumped onto his right shoulder. His eyes were shut, and he fell asleep.

The next evening, William was sitting on the edge of his bed, dressed in his school clothes, the sheets still tightly snug under the mattress. "Sir Thomas?" he asked.

"Is everything all right, William? Are you ill?"

"No, Sir Thomas. I've been wondering."

Thomas pulled the chair around so he could hold a conversation face to face. "I see," he started, fearful that another boy had said something to cause William's strange behavior, "what have you been wondering?"

"In the story, Sir Thomas—the one with the girl and the bzou . . . " He smiled, then continued. "How could the girl do all those horrible things the wolf told her to do and not realize how evil he was until it was almost too late?"

Before Thomas could think of an answer, William continued.

"You think maybe she is like the French people?"

Thomas rested his hands on his knees and stared at the child. The prior night he had been a bit irritated at William's giggling, feeling it was a sign of childish impertinence, but now the boy's question, asked in sincerity with no self-consciousness of its precocity, stunned him. He remembered William's peculiar facial expressions while he read to him the night before. "Is that what you were thinking last night while I was reading?"

William nodded.

"I'm curious," Thomas continued. "What made you connect the French people with the little girl?"

"You remember that night in the chapel? When you were playing the organ and you saw Timmy and me?"

"Yes."

"I showed you the list of French kings, and you told me that eventually there would be no king."

"Yes?"

"You told me that after there were no more kings, after the French people kicked them off the throne, they would eventually ask someone to lead them who had even more king-like power than the kings they kicked out of the country."

Thomas nodded. "That's right."

"It's Napoleon. Isn't it?"

Thomas felt his eyes widen and restrained himself from making any further facial movement. He did not want to show any reaction that may discourage William from such thoughts, and he certainly did not want to show any signs of being impressed by the child's logic, which could inflate the boy's ego. So, he consciously pressed his lips, kept his arms resting on his knees, and fixed his gaze on William.

Moments later, Thomas stood, put his hand on William's shoulder, and instructed him to put on his nightclothes.

He waited for William to pull the bedsheets up to his chin before he spoke again.

"William," he continued, "if there is something you'd like me to read, perhaps something we may not have at the school, just ask and I can try to find it at one of the libraries in the city; or one of the colleges."

William smiled, nestled his head into the pillow, and closed his eyes. "Thank you, Sir Thomas."

He walked to the entrance door of the dormitory, turned, and surveyed the expanse of beds and his fellow brothers scattered among the boys, still reading. It was odd for him to be one of the first to leave the dormitory. He saw William raise himself from the bed and look behind, searching. He raised his hand and waved at Thomas to come to his bedside.

"Yes, William, what is it?"

"Napoleon. I'd like to hear stories of Napoleon."

* * *

151

On the last day of June, Thomas received a telegram from BJ, inviting him to attend the championship games in October. BJ specifically asked that the boy William Jennings also attend.

The brothers granted the two-week leave to Thomas but were more reluctant to allow William to join. The previous year it was understandable, when the two friends were on the verge of being separated, but this year, allowing William to attend professional ball games when the other boys were in school may cause envy amongst the ranks.

Thomas showed the telegram to the other brothers so they could read BJ's specific request that William attend. They recognized that perhaps William's attendance could be classified as an apprenticeship outside the walls of St. Mary's—so they authorized his absence.

When Thomas informed William of the invitation, his face lit up. Under his bed he kept a sheet of paper with numbers in descending order from ninety-four to one, each number representing one less day to the start of the championship. Each evening, William would mark the highest number off the list. Before entering the dining commons for breakfast, he would search for Thomas or Brother Mathias or Brother Herman, hoping they had finished reading the morning paper. If he didn't obtain it then, he'd search for the same trio at lunch, and if not then, at dinner.

Prior to bedtime, William discussed the standings with Thomas and imagined which two cities they might travel to in October. The New York Giants were running away with the pennant in the National League. Being led by their aggressive manager, John McGraw, the team had a style of play resembling the powerhouse Orioles of the late 1890s when McGraw was a key player.

Since it appeared that Boston would repeat as American League champs, Thomas felt some hesitancy because he had become a close friend to McGraw at St. Bonaventure.

Once the study of standings and hypothetical discussions of train journeys ended, Thomas opened the cover of that evening's bedtime story. In the early summer months, he realized he could read excerpts from Tolstoy's *War and Peace* in which Napoleon made several appearances. He would always edit his reading, choosing beforehand what he believed would deliver the greatest punch of action, adventure, and insight into the character of the French emperor. He read a letter written by Napoleon to one of his marshals, Joachim Murat, declaring his disappointment for unauthorized action he took prior to the Battle of Austerlitz:

> I cannot find words to express to you my
> displeasure. You command only my advance
> guard and have no right to arrange an armistice
> without my order. You are causing me to lose
> the fruits of a campaign. Break the armistice
> immediately and march on the enemy . . .

He read of Prince Andrew Bolkonski encountering Napoleon after he had fallen wounded on the Austerlitz battlefield:

> Having gone a few steps he stopped before Prince Andrew, who lay on his back with the flagstaff that had been dropped beside him. "That's a fine death!" said Napoleon as he gazed at Bolkonski. Prince Andrew understood that this was said of him and that it was Napoleon who said it. He heard the speaker addressed as Sire. But he heard the words as he might have heard the buzzing of a fly . . . later . . . Prince Andrew had been brought forward before the Emperor to complete the show of prisoners . . . Napoleon apparently remembered seeing him on the battlefield . . . "Well, and you, young man . . . how do you feel?" . . . Prince Andrew, with his eyes fixed straight on Napoleon, was silent . . . so insignificant at that moment seemed to him all the interests that engrossed Napoleon . . . he could not answer him.

William listened attentively, always with wide eyes, sometimes smiling, sometimes stretching or propped up on the mattress, his arms wrapped around his legs, making it impossible to fall asleep.

Thomas had exhausted the *War and Peace* excerpts by the middle of July, including the defeated exodus of Napoleon and his diminished troops from Moscow. So Thomas decided to travel back in time. He went to Baltimore's library and found firsthand accounts and letters to Napoleon's marshals during his early campaigns in Egypt and the Middle East prior to his reign. He brought home accounts of battles against Spain, Austria, Prussia, and England following his rise as emperor. He read to William of his many victories won through the heroics of Marshall Ney and Marshall Soult; of his British nemeses, Horatio Nelson and Arthur Wellesley; his abdication and exile to the island of Elba. He read of his escape from Elba less than a year later and French troops embracing his return, allowing him to enter Paris without any opposition to resume his reign. He read about his final offensive against an allied force from England and Prussia that defeated him at a small village southwest of Brussels, forcing him to abdicate once more, this time exiled to St. Helena, an island far off the western coast of southern Africa.

Then there were the stories that had little to do with military exploits but were about the private life of the emperor. At the city library, Thomas found a set of letters compiled by a British writer, Lewis Goldsmith. Many questioned the historicity of the events that Goldsmith wrote in his *Memoirs of Court of St. Cloud*, but still, Thomas felt the stories were innocent enough to read to William.

In one account, Goldsmith describes an assassination attempt by chocolate:

> In his journey to be crowned King of Italy,
> Napoleon occupied his uncle's episcopal palace
> at Lyons during his forty-eight hours he
> remained there. Most of the persons composing
> the household were from Corsica; among these
> was a young woman by the name of Pauline
> Riotti, who inspected the economy of the
> kitchens. It was Bonaparte's custom to take a
> dish of chocolate in the forenoon, which she, on
> the morning of his departure, against her
> custom, but under the pretence of knowing the
> taste of the family, desired to prepare. One of
> the cooks observed that she mixed it with
> something from her pocket, but, without
> saying a word to her that indicated suspicion,
> he warned Bonaparte, in a note, delivered to a
> page, to be upon his guard. When the
> chamberlain carried in the chocolate, Napoleon
> ordered the person who had prepared it to be

> brought before him. This being told Pauline,
> she fainted away, after having first drunk the
> remaining contents of the chocolate pot. Her
> convulsions soon indicated that she was
> poisoned, and notwithstanding the endeavours
> of Bonaparte's physician, she expired within an
> hour; protesting that her crime was an act of
> revenge against Napoleon, who had . . .
> promised her marriage but since his elevation,
> had not only neglected her, but reduced her to
> despair by refusing an honest support for
> herself and her child.

Other stories of the emperor's close brushes with death by disgruntled subjects filled the late summer evenings into the early fall days of September. Thomas was learning details, historical and questionable, of French history he had never explored and was delving deeper than he would have had William not prompted him. In his studies he read several accounts of Napoleon's fascination with diamonds—apparently obsessed with the idea that the more audacious a jeweler's arrangement, the more legitimate the emperor would be seen in the estimation of his subjects and established European royalty. In 1801, about two years after becoming consul of France, he obtained the storied Regent diamond and commissioned a goldsmith to incorporate it into the sword he wore at his side. Ten years later, after divorcing Josephine because she did not bear him an heir, and after his new wife, Marie-Louise of Austria, gave birth to a son, he commissioned the creation of a silver and gold necklace made of 172 diamonds weighing 275 carats.

But perhaps none of these diamond exploits compared to the outrageous sequence of events surrounding a diamond necklace created about thirty years prior to Napoleon's reign—when King Louis XV still presided over the country. Because of the sordid actions by the characters involved, Thomas knew he could not read straight from the accounts written by Thomas Carlyle and Alexandre Dumas. So, he wrote a short summary of the events and read those to William one evening in late September:

> Once upon a time, King Louis XV of France wanted to
> show the woman he loved, Madame du Barry, how
> much he loved her—so he commissioned all the best
> jewelers in the kingdom to create a diamond necklace
> that would surpass all the other diamond necklaces
> that had ever been made. But before the necklace was
> finished, the king died.
>
> The jewelers were very frightened. Because they had
> spent so much money in gathering all the largest and
> most clear diamonds they could find, and since the king
> was dead, who could afford to buy the necklace? They

hoped that the king's son, Louis XVI, would want to purchase it for his beautiful wife, Marie Antoinette, but she did not want it.

There was a woman named Jeanne who was a distant relative of the new king and who was married to a police officer. She had a friend named Rohan—he was a cardinal in the Catholic church. The new queen did not like Rohan because they had many disagreements in the past, so Jeanne tried to help them make peace with one another. But secretly, she wanted something for herself.

Jeanne lied to her friend Rohan, saying that the queen wanted to meet him so that they could talk out their disagreements. But Jeanne found a young woman in France who resembled the queen and asked her to pretend to be Marie Antoinette. The woman convinced Rohan that she was the queen and that she was no longer upset with him. Over the next few months, Rohan received letters that were supposedly from the queen, expressing their new friendship. He was so happy to be friends once again with the queen of France. But the letters he was receiving were written by Jeanne—not the queen.

Eventually, the letters that Rohan was receiving began to request money to help the queen support some of her charity work throughout the country—but again, these were letters written by Jeanne. Rohan sent the money by messengers he believed were from the queen but were actually from Jeanne. Then, one day Jeanne came to see Rohan and tell him that the queen wanted him to buy the necklace that was commissioned by her father-in-law thirteen years earlier.

Rohan, who wanted to be a faithful friend to the queen, agreed. He negotiated a price with the jewelers for two million livres—that's over $500,000 for us.

Thomas looked over at William. His head was tilted forward, his eyes wide.

"What happened?" William whispered, "Did they get caught?"

Thomas continued:

After agreeing to make several payments for the balance owed, the jewelers handed Rohan the necklace. Jeanne had told him that a servant of the queen would be at the house waiting for his arrival. He should give the necklace to the servant, and the servant would bring it to the queen.

The servant, however, brought it to Jeanne's home and left.

Meanwhile, Jeanne's husband, the police officer, returned home from work, found the necklace, and immediately figured out what had happened. Without telling anybody, not even his wife, he took the necklace, traveled quickly north to Calais, boarded a ferry, and sold the necklace to a jeweler in England.

When the king and queen discovered what had happened, everybody was arrested and punished. However, it is believed that Jeanne's husband never returned to France, so nobody knows for sure what happened to the necklace. The common belief is that it was broken into pieces that were sold separately.

Whatever the story or account, all seemed to keep William spellbound. Anxious for Thomas to resume his reading from the night before, he was usually the first to dress in his nightclothes, first to wash, and first to be under the covers. However, if William was lying still, his arms folded across his chest, the morning edition of the *Baltimore Sun* under his arms, Thomas knew William was not in the mood for stories or history—he wanted to talk baseball. William would hold the paper folded lengthwise in his right hand, and underneath the Daily Edition he would be holding several white sheets of paper. The page on top was always the sheet with the numbers counting down the days until the two of them would depart for the 1904 championship. On the other sheets of paper were analyses of a variety of players in either league, analyses that closely resembled the "T-Reports" Thomas provided to BJ and the Boston Pilgrims a year earlier.

"What do you think?" he would ask when showing Thomas a chart of how to best pitch Honus Wagner or Napoleon Lajoie.

When William showed Thomas the sheet he created for Christy Mathewson, the young New York Giants pitcher, he chuckled. The items written on the paper were all strengths: tall, strong, smart, lots of pitches, good control of strike zone. The one weakness on the page was written as a question: "too nice?"

On Friday, September 30, on the top left corner of page nine of the *Baltimore Sun*'s morning edition, in bold print, was written, "Baseball's Fading Days." Underneath was a summary of the upcoming intracity postseason games that would be played between the teams that did not finish first in their league. These were exhibition games, played mostly for pride to boast that the respective team is the best in New York or Chicago or Philadelphia or St. Louis. But underneath this summary were listed the current standings, showing that the Giants had already won the National League and that the Pilgrims and Highlanders were battling back and forth to win the American League.

"So, it will be New York and Boston?" William asked.

"Yes," Thomas answered, attempting to suppress his uncertainty. The Giants had clearly already won the National League pennant, and the New York Highlanders also were still alive, fighting for the other league pennant against Boston, but what concerned Thomas was events transpiring off the field. He knew of the history between BJ and John McGraw. The Orioles had switched leagues in 1901, and McGraw was the natural man to lead the team in the American League. But as a manager, BJ often scolded him for his on-field tantrums and disrespect toward umpires. He knew BJ had frequently suspended McGraw for these episodes. McGraw left the American League Orioles club to manage the National League's Giants, thus escaping from under BJ's watchful eye. But BJ retaliated by moving the Baltimore team to New York, thereby erasing the monopoly the Giants held in Manhattan. Having spent two years with McGraw at St. Bonaventure, Thomas knew firsthand of his vindictive nature. He was not sure to what extent he may go to show his displeasure of BJ's treatment. On Friday, October 7, he found out.

In the middle of page nine, hidden between two other stories about the end of the baseball season, two short paragraphs confirmed Thomas's fear:

> Mr. John T. Brush, president of the New Yorks, the champions of the National League, has already declared that his club will not play any post-season games with the American League leaders or anybody else.

New York, Oct. 6. – There will be no post-season
series of games played this year between the
pennant winning teams of the National and
American Baseball Leagues. Manager John J.
McGraw, of the New York National League team,
said very emphatically tonight that he would not
play a post-season series.

When Thomas arrived at William's bedside that evening, he discovered William had already fallen asleep. The morning newspaper was crumpled and ripped and strewn under the bed. Beneath the scattered pieces of newspaper was a solitary sheet of white paper. On the front was the analysis table William had constructed for Emperor Napoleon, listing his strengths and weaknesses. Among the weaknesses were listed "stature, temper, and too many girlfriends." The strengths included "stature, loyalty, good leader, smart, good at math, wise generals (marshals)."

Thomas turned the sheet over. The top was entitled, "Little Napoleon."

Thomas glanced down toward William, figuring with all the sport columns the boy had read, that somewhere, William had learned that this was the preferred nickname sportswriters had given John McGraw. Underneath the title were written no strengths or weaknesses. Instead, there was a newspaper photograph of the Giants manager pasted to the middle of the page. In the picture McGraw was scowling, looking determined, wearing his uniform with *NY* on his cap and sleeve, hands on hips. William had drawn two horns on top of McGraw's cap and a tail protruding from McGraw's backside. Underneath the picture in bold capital letters, he had written the word *EVIL*.

Chapter 5

On isolated days when one of the other brothers became ill, Thomas cancelled the three one-hour music classes so he could attend to the apprenticeship training duties of the infirmed brother. The work performed by the boys impressed Thomas, whether it be at the cobbler shop, the ironworks, or the three-story clothing warehouse. Witnessing the children who struggled in class wielding tools of trades with confidence and efficiency was satisfying. It filled him with pride and hope that these boys faced a bright future and that he was contributing in some small way to shaping them into responsible citizens.

His favorite site to visit was the third floor of the clothing warehouse, where shirts of highest quality were handmade. He'd imagine all the bankers, lawyers, and accountants who would soon visit Baltimore department stores to purchase one of the shirts now being tailored by the boys of St. Mary's. William had left his musical pursuits over ten months earlier with the hopes of earning his way to the third floor. Just the fact that he was working at the tailor shop was noteworthy. Most of the other seven-year-olds were required to remain in the classroom after lunch, but William, whose reading skills surpassed most of the boys twice his age, would not benefit from the courses offered to the younger children after lunchtime.

Brother Paul had decided it would benefit William more if he could get a head start in learning a trade. After his eighth birthday, William was moved to the top floor.

Here he sewed buttons and stitched collars alongside his friends Congo and George. The three hours of work required concentration and attention to detail, but once a rhythm was reached, usually past the second hour of each day, the boys at some of the tables would begin to chatter amongst themselves or sing softly. Anything to break the monotony.

Thomas raised his eyes from the music arrangements he was considering for a fall concert when he heard a faint, stilted whisper chanting a familiar tune:

> 'Tis you who makes my friends my foes,
> 'Tis you who makes me wear old clothes;
> Here you are, so near my nose,
> So tip her up, and down she goes.

As the solitary voice sang, the volume increased. Congo and William raised their heads from their work and smiled as George began the chorus:

> Ha, ha, ha, you and me,
> Little brown jug, don't I love thee!
> Ha, ha, ha, you and me,
> Little brown jug, don't I love thee!

Congo and William soon joined:

> When I go toiling to my farm,
> I take little brown jug under my arm;
> I place it under a shady tree,
> Little brown jug, 'tis you and me.

And then the other tables joined, creating a harmony:

> Ha, Ha, Ha, you and me,
> Little brown jug, don't I love thee!
> Ha, ha, ha, you and me,
> Little brown jug, don't I love thee!

"Hurrah! Hurrah!" isolated voices shouted from tables across the floor.

Congo, George, and William turned toward Thomas, as if they feared his disapproval. But Thomas raised his hand and smiled, gesturing them to continue by twirling his hand in circles several times.

"Where'd you learn all these songs, George?" Thomas heard William ask as he struggled to thread a needle through a button.

"Ha!" Congo blurted, then hunched his shoulders and leaned close to William, "Hasn't he told you?"

William shook his head.

Congo cupped his hands around William's left ear and whispered.

William's eyes widened.

"Kid," George said softly as he stitched the collar of a shirt. "I come from an unsavory lot. Raised in a tavern. They couldn't control me. So they dropped my ugly body at the front gate of this fine institution."

"So . . . so . . . " William started, somewhat excited. "You have . . . I mean . . . "

Congo and George looked at one another, smiling, apparently finding it funny that William struggled to find correct words to ask what he wanted.

"You know your parents?" William asked.

"Don't think it's an advantage, Kid," George said while sewing a button on the shirt's lapel. "They never come to see me." He raised his hands and passed them over his body. "Ain't anything special for them to come see . . . eh?"

As George continued working, Congo and William stopped their sewing, looking at George with what appeared as brotherly compassion.

"George?" William said softly. "Is that why you play catcher every day?"

George looked up, his eyes narrowed and focused on William. "What's that?" he said. He stood and walked to William's side, shoving him on the shoulder. "What do you think you know about it, Kid?"

Before Thomas could intervene, Congo ran between his two friends and held out his arms, holding George by the collar with his left hand, his right resting softly on William's shoulder.

"Kid didn't mean anything by it, George. Did you, William?

William dropped his work and placed his hands over his eyes.

"Look," Congo said to George. "He's sorry. Didn't mean anything by it."

George turned to face Congo. He stood on the tips of his toes so he was now equal in height to his friend. "I catch because I call the best game," George stated, pointing his index finger at Congo, then digging it into his friend's chest. "I catch because I can throw the quickest to second." He placed both hands on Congo's chest and pushed him away with enough force that it sent Congo to the floor. He stood over Congo and pointed at himself. "I don't catch so that some stupid mask hides this hideous face."

George returned to his seat, picked up the shirt he had been working on, and continued threading. As Congo returned to his seat, he and William were looking at one another. It seemed to Thomas that somehow their eyes were communicating. It seemed perhaps a tipping point had been reached, and the two friends were about to embark on a plan.

* * *

Letter Addressed to: Alexander Chalmers
103 Orchard Street, New York, NY
Postmarked: Baltimore, Maryland; September 1, 1905

Dear Alexander,

Thank you for your hospitality this past summer. Those two weeks provided me with rest, retreat, and the opportunity to become acquainted with your family. You and Sarah have done well. I recall that when you were newly married, each of you feared the challenges of raising children, but from my perspective the kids in your home are treasures—the two of you ought to be proud. Ruth is already a young woman, beautiful and helpful around the home. Eli is a rascal but has a solid heart, and I imagine he will be a blessing to you as he ages. The twins are precious—their smiles and laughter and singing and dancing add to the cheerfulness of your home. Though David is still a toddler, I see an anticipation in his eyes as he observes the activity in your home from his crib, anxious for the day he can join his siblings in their adventures.

Upon my return to the school, I have been pleasantly surprised by both the eagerness of the boys in music class as well as the improvement in their skills and the sound they are producing as a unit. I had forgotten how wonderful the feeling to be a member of a team that creates melody. It is even more uplifting for me as the director since I am now able to witness on the boys' faces the pride they feel when the sound coming from their instruments is clear, robust, and unified. The progress they have made in one year has pleased all of us, not only because the performances throughout Baltimore have brought a certain prestigious pride upon St. Mary's, but also because the performance and behavior of the boys has improved in their other coursework. In all, the way things have transpired over the past six to seven years leaves me speechless and grateful—I could not have orchestrated things in my life to be at a better place than they are now. Master of the Universe is faithful!

The main purpose in my writing is to extend an invitation. As we discussed during my time in New York, Mr. Johnson has again asked me to attend the games that will be played in October. Although it is still not clear which teams will be participating, I am fairly certain that your Giants will be representing the National League. Mr. McGraw has deservedly received bad publicity in your city and around the nation for his refusal to play Boston last year, and I have read that he has already guaranteed the Giants will play in this year's contest. Therefore, if New York does win the National League pennant, I would like to invite you to join me at the games played at the Polo Grounds.

Mr. Johnson has further asked me to bring William to all the games. I had shared with you that it was William who discovered Phillippe's foot placement on the rubber two years ago. As a result, BJ has it set in his mind that William is a boy genius, or perhaps a good luck charm, and has offered to pay for both our tickets—and graciously agreed to pay for three tickets for any games played at the Polo Grounds.

During our lunch on the day I left, we had discussed the prospect of disclosing to William the pieces of his past that you know. I suspect there is much that you have not revealed to me simply because you have not wanted to put me in the position of determining when and how much to tell him. As I told you that day, William is a bright boy, and though he has not yet asked me or any of the brothers of his past, I am certain that questions are dancing through his mind.

Why, just this past week, I saw William break down in tears as he and two other boys spoke of their families when working in the tailor shop. The other boys are both about two years older than William. After George, the elder of William's two friends, and Congo almost got in a fight, I noticed a peculiar expression pass between William and Congo. I wondered what it meant and found out earlier today.

During today's ball game on the Little Field, Congo was pitching horribly. On a normal day, he may give up a base on balls or a single every other inning—the other team may score one run, or two at most, during a six-inning game. But today, the other team had scored six runs in the first inning and another three in the second. And after two runs had already been scored in the third, Brother Mathias walked to the mound, and as Congo handed the ball to Mathias, George, who was playing catcher, shouted, "It's about time! Finally!" Mathias turned toward George and held up his hand, instructing him to be quiet. Then he beckoned William from his second base position and handed the ball to him. William has developed a nasty curveball, and though he is young and small in stature, he has a pretty fast straight ball also. These two pitches have made him the second-best pitcher amongst the younger boys.

William fared no better than Congo. In fact, he performed worse—did not retire one batter—and gave up ten additional runs. All the while, George's comments from behind the plate began to grow in volume and derisiveness.

"Crap, Kid. What you throwing? A two-year-old girl can hit those pitches!"

"Now pitching—the kid who can't get the worst batsman in Baltimore out!"

"You've all heard of Cracker Jacks? Well, out there on the mound we have a kid who couldn't get a cracker out!"

Finally, Brother Mathias, whose frustration was clear, beckoned me to go speak to him.

"Is something wrong, William?" I asked. "Is your arm sore?"

He responded by asking me a question. "Have you ever played catch with George?" Before I could answer, he continued. "It stings my hand, even when he is just tossing the ball back to me from behind the plate."

I wasn't able to think of what to say in response, and then George began to spout more dialogue. "Don't waste your time with him, Brother Thomas. He's as done as a burnt steak!" William smiled and looked up at me. "How much longer you think Brother M puts up with this?"

Then suddenly, I heard Mathius clap his hands loudly and shout in exasperation, "That's enough!" He marched to the mound, took the ball from William, and shouted at George. "Take that mask off and get out here!"

*Not one batsman on the opposing team reached base safely
the rest of the game. All but two of the outs recorded by
George were by strikeout. Side by side on the bench, smiling
and giving each other celebratory shoves with each of
George's outs, were Congo and William. I write this detailed
account to let you know that the wheels in William's head are
turning—finely tuned and oiled. Please consider what steps we
can take to lessen the potential hurt the boy will experience
upon learning of his history. Better to know the facts, as few as
we know, than to allow him to imagine how horrible his story
may be.*

Give my regards to Sarah and the children.

Blessings,

Thomas

Letter Addressed to: Brother Thomas Kemp

St. Mary's Industrial School for Boys, Baltimore, MD

Postmarked: New York, NY; September 12, 1905

Dear Thomas,

Thank you for your letter. I have read it to Sarah, and we are grateful for your kind words. We enjoyed your visit and hope to see you again soon. The kids are well—all six of them. That's right, we discovered a week after you left that Sarah is with child.

I concur with your assessment of the Giants' likelihood to play in this year's championship—therefore I heartily accept your invitation. My hope is that Connie Mack's Athletics will win the other pennant and we can see the two geniuses compete.

With regard to William, I also concur with your assessment. A day does not go by that I do not think of him and wonder when or how we can help him navigate through the scant details we can offer. Not sure what exactly I will say or how much I ought to reveal. I plan to talk it over with Sarah, ask for the Muster's wisdom, and seek advice from our old friend Nathan who just returned from one of his Dakota sabbaticals.

I wished he were here last month so the three of us could have spent time together and reminisced of our days in Chicago, but alas, we can do that when you come in October. Ever since he spent time out West back in the mid-80s, before we met him at the Great Fair, he embraced the rancher culture and prides himself as a genuine cowboy. I think it helps him recapture some of that energy he once held in such excess. When we met him in Chicago, though he was the eldest of the four of us, he was the one who worked the most hours, worked with the greatest vigor, and took the greatest risk when our bosses asked for volunteers. Even now, somewhere in his mid-fifties (Sarah doesn't even know his exact age), he exuberantly marches into new ventures and jobs and responsibilities. I smile as I try to piece together his life: from somewhere in western Russia, traveling west as a young rabbi, ending up in Italy, and leaving port from Naples. Making port in New York, odd jobs working in jewelry shops and helping with readings at synagogue filling his years. He even assisted Riis with his book, thereby picking up some photography skills, until he moved out West and met Roosevelt. Then, missing the city, he travels east to Chicago and joins the construction crew for the Great Fair. When Roosevelt becomes police chief, he tracks Nate down and asks him to join the force to help with the escalating crime in the overcrowded tenement homes on the East Side. That's of course when I follow him to the city, and he introduces me to his niece. Once Sarah and I start our family, Nate stays close at first. Then during the war, he joins Roosevelt's Rough Riders in Cuba. Around the time Roosevelt takes office, he leaves for Kentucky to start some venture with a fellow Rider and eventually leaves with some wealth. He travels back west to Dakota and purchases a ranch. We receive an occasional letter, letting us know that he is still living. Always an entertaining read after supper around the table, just glad to have him back "home."

I didn't intend to go on about Uncle Nate, but I do find myself living vicariously through his adventures. Just writing about him tickles my imagination. I hesitate to ask his advice about William. From prior experience, he may just stare back at me with a blank expression, or he may tell me that it is hopeless to think anything can be done for the boy—"If he's meant to rise above his lot, then so be it. If he isn't, there ain't nothing you or me or Thomas and the other brothers can do."

So, yes, Thomas. We will talk. Look forward to seeing you and meeting William again.

Many blessings to you all.

Alex

***

After morning mass on Sunday, October 8, Thomas and William waited with their luggage outside the white picket fence of St. Mary's for the next streetcar to Union Station. From Union, they traveled two hours north to Philadelphia's Broad Street Station and checked in to their hotel several blocks away from Columbia Park, the home of the American League's Athletics.

William had not spoken much during the trip. He seemed conflicted. After the Giants refused to play in the championship one year earlier, he had vowed to no longer follow the progress of the season. In April, after opening day, he didn't ask for the morning edition of the *Baltimore Daily News*. No longer checking the standings or reading the sports editorials or recording the statistics of his favorite players, he had more time to read and study and improve his own playing skills on the Little Field. But the other boys talked, and it was inevitable that William's curiosity would be sparked. When he learned that the Giants' Christy Mathewson was winning almost each game he started, he asked Thomas if he thought Matty was the best pitcher ever. When he heard George and Congo speak of the batting prowess of Wagner and Lajoie and a rookie in Detroit named Cobb, he again sought Thomas's opinion.

In the end, his love of the game was stronger than his determination to prove his hatred for McGraw. When Thomas informed him of BJ's invitation, his eyes raised and fixed on Thomas. "We get to see Matty pitch?" And although Thomas was also excited to see the great pitcher, his task would be to find some flaw in Mathewson's delivery that Connie Mack's Athletics could exploit.

The ball games were not the primary concern of Thomas. For the past month, ever since he received Alexander's letter, he thought of the task before them. He decided to say nothing to William—did not want to raise any expectation or fear.

The spectacle of peripheral activities dominated the first game of the championship. Five hundred fans from New York sat near the Giants dugout on the first base side. A small band among them played "Tammany" and "Give My Regards to Broadway" as the Giants took the field and stretched and played catch with one another. The Giants uniforms were brand new—black pants and tops with a bold white "NY" in the middle of the chest, and white hats, white belts, and white stockings. The fans tried to outshout their opponents. "Johnnie get cher gun, my son, we've won . . . Johnnie get cher gun. It's ten to one," the New York fans shouted when McGraw walked near them. The Philadelphia fans shouted support for their skipper: "Connie Mack, Crack-a-Jack."

Just before the game was scheduled to begin, as the umpires met with McGraw and Athletics captain, Lave Cross, Thomas heard a hush and isolated pockets of laughter. Lave Cross approached the plate with his arms held behind his back. When the umpires finished discussing ground rules, Cross reached out his arms, revealing a strange, out-of-place porcelain figurine. Upon closer examination, Thomas recognized the figure to be an elephant about the size of two handbreadths, atop a thin bright green pedestal. Once Cross handed McGraw the elephant, he leaned forward, a smile growing with each passing moment, his eyes studying McGraw, hoping, it seemed, that the gesture would be greeted with amusement. The Giants manager held the elephant in both hands, studying it, smiling and laughing with the crowd. Even the home plate umpire, Jack Sheridan, looked on with what appeared to be suppressed amusement, his head tilted, admiring the elephant held by McGraw.

William was shifting his balance from his left foot to his right. He seemed excited, as if he appreciated the ceremony. And Thomas wondered how someone William's age could appreciate the humor displayed at the plate.

Three years prior to this meeting, when the American League was in its infancy and the Athletics were a young team, reporters asked McGraw his opinion of Mack's Athletics. "White elephants!" McGraw had replied. "Mr. Shibe has a white elephant on his hands."

The elephant became the mascot of the franchise, a rallying point, a way for the players, the fans, and the city to embrace their hapless team. And when the players responded by winning the pennant, the image stuck. Now, the team with the chance of a white elephant was playing the manager who so easily dismissed their acumen. From McGraw's reaction, he also seemed to appreciate the irony of the moment. He tipped his hat to the crowd, bowed, then held high the elephant and posed for several photographers. Finally, just before he turned to walk back toward his bench, McGraw stepped toward the Athletics dugout, and once the Athletics manager,

Connie Mack, dressed in his gray flannel suit and business hat, saw McGraw staring in his direction, the two baseball geniuses acknowledged one another—McGraw by touching the bill of his cap, Mack by touching the tip of his fedora.

"You think the elephant is funny?" Thomas shouted to William over the noise of the crowd.

William shrugged. "They're sticking it to McGraw for what he said three years ago!"

Thomas nodded, convinced William did understand the ironic ceremony.

When the Giants catcher and leadoff hitter, Roger Bresnahan, led the top of the fifth inning with a single, then stole second, a fan stood in the midst of the five hundred New Yorkers, holding high a large light-yellowish piece of butcher paper. One of his friends wrote on the paper with charcoal, "Roger, thou artful dodger, they catch thee not!" Later in the inning, when Giants slugger Mike Donlin swung and missed a juicy pitch, the same two wrote on a new piece of paper, "What! A strike on our Mike? It cannot be!" Then, on the next pitch, Donlin smacked a clean line drive into left field, scoring the Giants' first run.

The remainder of the game held little drama. New York scored two runs in the fifth and one in the top of the ninth. Mathewson scattered four hits and walked none. The greatest offensive threat the Athletics managed to create was in the bottom of the fifth when the right fielder, Socks Seybold, led the inning by hitting a sharp line drive that hit Mathewson in the stomach. Matty didn't flinch. He retrieved the ball and threw to first, retiring Seybold. McGraw rushed out, checking on Matty's status. Matty reluctantly left the field and went to the Giants bench to be examined by the training staff. He returned to the mound several minutes later and resumed his dominance. During that interval, there was an eerie quiet throughout Columbia Park. Most of the crowd, Thomas assumed, felt what he did, a mixture of hope and dismay: hope that Matty would not return so that their team had a fighting chance to get back into the game, and dismay that the most beloved player in either league had been injured and the brilliant display of his skills had ended for the day.

William was on the edge of his seat during that interval, his hands gripping the railing in front of him, his eyes focusing on the Giants bench. When Matty jogged back to the mound, William sat back in his seat. "Whew!" he said softly.

The next game was to be played the following day in New York. So, once Mathewson finished his complete game shutout, beating the Athletics 3–0, Thomas and William rushed to the hotel, picked up their luggage, walked to the nearby train depot, and boarded an early evening train to Manhattan. They arrived at Grand Central Station just after seven, then boarded a coach that transported them to the Astor Hotel.

Though the Astor had lost some of the prestige it held during the middle of the nineteenth century, Thomas was looking forward to spending a few days within its embrace. When they checked in at the front desk, Thomas hoped a telegram from Alexander would be waiting, explaining where and when the three of them would meet the following morning.

After Thomas signed the guest register, the clerk searched the cubby holes behind him. He reached into a space on the top row and grabbed the telegram addressed to Thomas.

"For you, Mr. Kemp," he said.

Thomas nodded. "Thank you."

He opened and read:

NEW YORK NEW YORK, 127P OCT 09 1905

THOMAS KEMP

ASTOR HOTEL, NEW YORK, NY

URGENT <STOP>

DO NOT GO TO ORCHARD STREET <STOP>

ALEX UNABLE TO ATTEND GAME <STOP>

MEET ME AT BIALYSTOKER TOMORROW AT 10 <STOP>

NATHANIEL MARSH

Thomas looked up from the telegram. The hotel clerk seemed to be waiting. "Is everything all right, Mr. Kemp?"

"I'm not sure."

Still holding the telegram, he reached down for their luggage, turned and walked toward the lobby, looking behind to be sure William was following, and placed the luggage at the foot of a set of cushioned chairs. "Sit here, William," he instructed.

Thomas read the telegram once more, struggling to make sense of it. Why was Nathan warning him not to go to Alex's home? What had happened?

"Sir Thomas," William whispered.

He read it a third time, sensing something horrible had occurred.

William stood and reached for Thomas's shoulder, tapping it softly and whispering again, "Sir Thomas."

Thomas was irritated. His plans had been sabotaged. He looked down at William and wanted to scold him for interrupting his attempt to make sense of it all.

"What!" he said sharply. "What is it, William?"

The boy stepped back, raised his arm, and pointed to someone behind them.

It was the clerk.

"Mr. Kemp." The clerk sounded apologetic and extended his hand that held an envelope. "I was reminded by one of the pages that a messenger left this for you earlier today."

Thomas reached out and immediately recognized the handwriting. Several years earlier at St. Bonaventure, he had read and edited countless essays from the man who had scribbled his name on the face of the envelope he now held. He pressed his eyes, feeling another wave of overwhelm approaching.

He hadn't had ample time to digest the news about Alexander, and now he dreaded reading the message that John McGraw had written:

> *Thomas,*
>
> *When I learned of your situation and attendance at*
> *the championship games, I felt compelled to write.*
>
> *We must talk.*
>
> *I will be in the lobby later tonight.*
>
> *J. M.*

* * *

The following morning they walked to the subway entrance at Broadway and 42nd, boarded the eastbound train, and exited at Canal.

Thomas had not gone to the lobby the previous evening. He had no intention of meeting McGraw, no intention of offering the least bit of encouragement, for he was confident of McGraw's intentions.

Thomas reached for William's hand, walked across the street toward a policeman, and asked directions to Bialystoker, the synagogue at which they were to meet Nathan.

"Walk toward the bridge," the officer said as he pointed east toward the towering steel structure. "It's between Grand and Delancey, about two blocks from the river."

"Is that the Brooklyn Bridge?" William asked.

"No, it is not," the officer answered. "Williamsburg Bridge, that is. Opened two years ago. It's something, ain't it?"

"Yes, sir." William frowned.

The officer pointed southward. "Over there, if you look close on a clear day, you can see the Brooklyn Bridge."

"Thank you, Officer." Thomas placed his hand on William's shoulder and turned him toward the direction they needed to travel. "How far?" he asked.

"About a mile. Take you 'bout twenty minutes."

Thomas reached into the pocket of his cassock and looked at his watch. It was 9:30. He'd discover soon whatever news awaited him. Then he'd make the journey back toward the hotel and head north to the Polo

Grounds, a journey he hoped to make in time for the three o'clock start of game two and avoid any chance encounter with McGraw.

When they reached what looked to be a synagogue, Thomas stopped at the steps and looked up. William did the same. Though not as majestic as the Williamsburg Bridge just to their right, the structure held them both in a momentary pause. It was as if they were at an art museum and stood before a fine painting.

"Is this it?" William asked.

It was a stone building of simple Federal design. Its original construction did not appear to be for those of the Jewish faith—instead, it was likely built for a Methodist or Episcopalian congregation. In place of a cross, on the roof was a bronze Star of David. Three stained glass windows were positioned symmetrically above three entrance doors. Near the top of the center window was another Star of David.

William looked up at Thomas. "Is this a church?"

"It's a synagogue. People who are of the Jewish faith worship here."

"So, it's like a church?"

"That's right," Thomas answered as he stepped onto the bottom step.

William pointed to the bright white star on the center window. "What's that?"

"You've heard of King David?"

"The boy who killed the giant?"

"Yes. It's named after him. It's the Star of David, the symbol of God's faithfulness."

Thomas walked up the stairs to the center door.

"Thomas!" a voice from below called out. "Thomas Kemp."

Turning, he bumped into William, causing him to lose his balance. He grabbed William's shoulder to prevent him from falling down the steps.

Ascending a stairway on the right edge of the synagogue was a man dressed in black pants, a black coat, and a rounded black felt hat. Underneath the coat was a worn and somewhat untucked white shirt, the buttons slightly off center. The man's beard was cleanly shaven, the hair under his hat thick and wild. He was broad shouldered and a bit heavier than ten years earlier—the last time Thomas had seen him.

"Thomas," Nathan Marsh said as he beckoned. "This way." He motioned for them to follow him down the stairs.

"The front entrance is for congregants," Nathan said, "on Sabbat and high days." He walked to the door at the bottom of the stairwell, opened it, and held it just long enough for Thomas to grab the handle on the inside. Then he turned and started walking down the hall lined with small offices on the left side and scattered benches against the right. Each office had a window and was scantly furnished.

Nathaniel spoke over his shoulder. "These are the offices for the rabbi." He pointed at the larger of the offices on the left. "And for the school's teachers," he said, pointing toward the second set of offices. "The others are for support staff." He spread his arms wide. "And finally, this is my office." He stopped at the end of the corridor. Nathan was the only one in office – Thomas wondered if the other occupants were working elsewhere, teaching perhaps, and if this was normal for him to be the only one working at this time of the day.

The door was already open. Nathan held his arm out, inviting Thomas to walk inside. "You can sit there, Thomas." He pointed at a solitary chair on one side of a very small, very old wooden desk. "The boy can wait in the hall on the bench."

Thomas had forgotten, or maybe he just hoped things had changed. But Nathan had not changed. He was still gruff and a bit rude. He hadn't yet made eye contact with Thomas, hadn't reached out for a handshake, hadn't asked to be introduced to William. He seemed intent on getting done as quickly as possible—whatever it was that had to be done.

"Nathaniel," Thomas said with a hopeful smile, "it's good to see you." He held out his arms, anticipating a hug.

Nathan lowered his head, and in what appeared to be genuine shame, shook his head in frustration. "I'm sorry, Thomas," he offered. "It's with everything that's happened the past few days . . . I don't know . . . I'm not sure . . . what to do."

And instead of responding to Thomas's open arms with a hug, instead of extending his hand for a handshake, he shut the office door, walked to the chair behind his desk, and dropped himself down onto the worn upholstery. He propped his head on his hands, his elbows bracing the weight.

Thomas slowly sat. He looked over his shoulder at William, sitting on one of the wooden benches, his eyes wide, his head tilted upward.

Thomas turned back toward his friend. Nathan covered his face with his hands, then rubbed his eyes, and moments later scratched his beard. He looked down at some papers scattered on his desk and sighed. "Thomas, the family is sick."

Thomas waited, anticipating more information.

"All of them . . . well, almost all of them. Sarah is okay. Said she had the illness when she was a child back in Poland. Doctor says that's why she's not affected. Suppose it's a blessing—yes? She's able to care for—"

"Nathan," Thomas interrupted, "slow down. Sick?"

"Measles. First it was Eli, next day the twins . . . then little David. Next Ruth . . . now Alex. The doctor quarantined the whole building—nobody in, nobody out."

Thomas had come to New York with an agenda: a hope that William and Alexander would meet and perhaps have a conversation. But Nathan's news made that impossible.

Nathan continued. "There's a placard posted on all the entrances stating that any person entering or leaving without permission of the health department is in violation of the law."

"How long?" Thomas asked.

"At least a week. Maybe two."

Thomas breathed deep. He looked behind to check on William, who was still seated on the bench, his eyes communicating concern.

"If it's any consolation," Nathan went on, "the family sends their greetings."

Nathan's words had all been spoken in monotone, with no indication he felt any empathy for Thomas, for William, or for any of those suffering from the illness.

Thomas had grown accustomed to this apparent indifference during their year of service in Chicago. It wasn't that Nathan didn't care—he cared so much that he grew overwhelmed by the problems others experienced, guilt-ridden that he was incapable of assisting them. He felt terrible that his paralyzing guilt prevented him from making any attempts to assist, that he had little energy left to show any outward display of sympathy. Eventually the weight of emotion would break, and Nathan would become an uncontrollable jumble of tears and sobs.

"How are you holding up, Nate?" Thomas asked.

Nathan lowered his eyes, shook his head, and shrugged his shoulders. "Helpless," he muttered.

Tears formed in the corners of Nathan's eyes and began to glisten on his dark beard. He swiped his sleeve under his nose and sniffled.

He bent down to open a drawer of his desk and reached for a folder. "Look at this," he said as he held the folder, waiting for Thomas to grab it.

Thomas opened the folder. "What am I looking at?"

"Six, seven years ago—I don't remember exactly. Before the twins were born, Alexander asked me to do something."

"And in this folder is what he asked of you?" Thomas asked.

"Look at the first page, the date it was prepared."

Thomas glanced at the top page and read, "September 30, 1905."

Nathan sighed, shifted in his chair, and ran his hand down his beard. He looked up at Thomas with shoulders slouched. "Ten days ago, Thomas—ten days ago. A task Alexander has been waiting six years for me to accomplish, I performed ten days ago."

Curious as to what could take Nathan six years to accomplish, Thomas looked at the papers more closely. The top page was a legal document signed by Nathan and another man whose name he did not recognize. The second page also was signed by Nathan and a second individual, also a name Thomas did not recognize. All ten pages were written in legal terms and signed by two individuals—Nathaniel Marsh and one other person with whom Thomas was not familiar.

It seemed most of the words on each page were unnecessary—but legal documents were like that. In the midst of all the words, near the center of each page a dollar amount was typed. Thomas thumbed back and forth through the pages, quickly cataloging the amounts: $49,000, $42,000, $63,000, $57,000, $76,000. He looked up at Nathan, then back at the pages. The words immediately prior to each dollar amount read, "The estimated value of the three stones is . . ."

"What is this?" Thomas asked, holding up the folder and papers.

"Diamonds," Nathan answered. "Alex asked me to value them when he returned from Baltimore, after he left the child with you and the brothers."

"Diamonds?"

Nathan nodded. "They were found with the boy on the ship. Stitched into his blanket."

Thomas studied Nathan, wondering if his friend was weaving one of his intricate tales that held little to no truth. But Nathan was not grinning, not showing signs of suppressing a smile.

"Alexander said nothing of this to you?" Nathan asked.

Thomas turned quickly, looking at William. He wondered if the boy was aware that he was the topic of conversation.

He turned back to face Nathan. "Nothing."

"Well," Nathan continued, "he wanted me to get confirmation. Proof of the stones' value. 'Get as many second opinions as possible,' he instructed. I was struck immediately by the quality and clarity, felt an urgency to place them in a protected location, so we rented a box at a bank on Wall Street, but I never got around to getting those other opinions—until, well, you see the letters."

Thomas was annoyed at Alexander, then realized this was only one piece of information about William's history that had been withheld. In the past, Thomas had been grateful to Alexander for revealing little detail—grateful he had nothing to tell William if or when he asked him.

He had hoped William could meet Alexander. He had hoped Alexander could be a source for William to go to when he had questions about his heritage. But that was not to be on this trip. Alexander would not be able to attend the game with them.

"Nathan?" Thomas asked.

His friend looked up.

"What is your schedule today?"

Nathan rubbed his beard. He pointed at the stack of papers on his desk. "These are recent immigrants—Russian, Hungarian, German—stranded on Ellis. I'm helping the staff expedite their applications for release."

"Not today," Thomas protested. "You're coming with us to the game."

"With you and the boy?" Nathan whispered.

"Yes."

Nathan sat straight. He appeared to consider the possibility. He smiled. Then frowned. "Do I have to speak to the boy?"

* * *

The atmosphere at the Polo Grounds was circus-like. Whereas the Giants wore black tops and pants in Philadelphia, now, as the home team, they wore white.

One hour prior to the scheduled first pitch there were fans in the outfield, behind ropes set up by the New York Police Department. Thomas guessed the crowd behind each rope was twenty to thirty people deep. Still, streams of fans entered. Men and women, young and old, jumped from one aisle to the next, leaping or climbing over seats, trying to get a better view of pregame festivities. Behind the Polo Grounds' home plate façade, where VIPs and reporters had prime seating locations, rose Coogan's Bluff, the huge granite rock formation that offered the more daring nonpaying Giants fans a bird's-eye view of the activity below them. The top of the bluff was full of fans. It seemed to Thomas a dangerous place to watch a game. He feared at some point a fan may topple from the bluff onto the roof of the stadium.

Some fans were blowing trumpets. Others were blowing whistles, and some held cowbells in one hand, rattles in the other. The resulting cacophony bordered somewhere between the eerie and the joyful. Any concern, Thomas thought, that Nathan had of having to converse with

William during the nine-inning game was being erased by the chaos around them.

Ban Johnson had again procured good seats—just left of center, behind home plate. The New York fans paid little attention to Thomas, William, and Nathan, stepping on their feet and elbowing them in the face. There was an occasional "excuse me" offered, but for the most part, Thomas felt it was a similar experience to what he faced on the city's elevated trains when the cars were full to capacity. "Excuse me" was not necessary in such circumstances.

"Look at that," Thomas heard William shout. "Somebody just threw a straw hat onto the field!"

William was standing on top of his seat, pointing at the white hat. One of the players bent over and picked it up. He was a handsome young man with a strong nose and jaw. He was tall and slim. He looked at the hat with what seemed to Thomas a playful stare, removed his ball cap, placed the white straw hat atop his head, and tipped the bill, smiling at nearby fans.

"Is that Rube Waddell?" William asked excitedly, turning toward Thomas. "Is that him?"

Thomas was not certain, for he had never seen Waddell pitch, but he guessed from the events occurring before them that it must be the dominant southpaw. "I think so," he answered.

"Who's Rube Waddell?" Nathan asked.

Thomas turned his head, making sure it was Nathan who asked the question. Nathan looked back at Thomas with an expression of curiosity.

"Rube Waddell?" William shouted. He jumped off the seat and landed in front of Nathan. The noise of the crowd had not subsided, so the conversation between the three of them was shouted more than spoken.

"Who is Rube Waddell?" William repeated. "Next to Matty, he is the best pitcher in either league! He won twenty-seven games this year, had a 1.48 ERA, and struck out 287 batters—and over three hundred batters in both of the previous seasons!"

"And the straw hat?" Nathan asked with a faint grin.

William's shoulders dropped, as if Nathan's question diffused the great pitcher's statistics. "He got in a fight with one of his teammates. Took off his hat as they were waiting for a train. Somehow, as they were fighting, he banged his arm against the side of the train and hurt his arm."

"Maybe," Thomas added once William finished his explanation.

William turned immediately, a look of fear that perhaps what he had just said was not entirely accurate.

Nathan inched forward in his seat and turned toward Thomas.

Thomas paused, surprised to see an excited smile growing on his friend's face.

"The more likely scenario," Thomas continued, "is that Connie Mack got tired of his childish, undisciplined behavior and will not let him play for the series."

"You mean like a punishment?" William asked.

"No hint of gamblers influencing the young player?" Nathan asked simultaneously.

Thomas shook his head and pursed his lips, trying to communicate to Nathan to stop any line of discussion regarding the rumors surrounding Waddell's association with the gambling underworld. As of yet, William was not aware of such a reality, and Thomas hoped to keep the boy free from such knowledge.

As the Giants took the field, a band started playing "Give My Regards to Broadway."

"Now, McGraw! Go get 'em!" a fan shouted.

Another followed. "Go get 'em, Mike! Go get 'em, Dan!"

And, "You, Roger! You know how to do it! Fix 'em!"

In the top of the first, Joe McGinnity, the Giants pitcher, did "fix 'em." Although Philadelphia's leadoff hitter, Topsy Hartsel, hit a clean single, he was erased on a fielder's choice, and nobody else reached base.

As the Giants rushed to their dugout and the Athletics ran to their positions, the noise of the crowd subsided. William tapped Thomas in the side and asked, "Waddell was punished? But why would Connie Mack do that? He's their best pitcher!"

Thomas was writing a summary of McGinnity's pitch sequence when William asked the question. He placed his writing pad on his lap and closed the pen. "If you or one of the boys breaks one of the rules, what happens?"

William answered quickly and with sadness. "We don't get to play ball for one or two days."

"And how does this punishment affect future behavior?"

William placed his arm under his chin. "But he's not a boy."

"We'll see," Thomas said, as the bottom of the first began.

Since Waddell was not available to pitch and Eddie Plank had pitched in the first game, Connie Mack used his next best pitcher, Charles Bender.

"Heap much, Chief!" a fan shouted. "Get 'em!" And then after mimicking the sound of a beating drum, the fan repeated in a chant, "Heap much, Chief!"

The fan continued his chant, intermingled with his impersonation of a beating drum. Other fans joined, mimicking variations of Indian war cries, mocking the Native American heritage of the Athletics pitcher.

Roger Bresnahan led the inning off with a double, but Bender retired the next three hitters.

Both teams did little at the plate. The noise in the stadium became a whisper compared to the volume prior to the game's start.

"Do you know much about baseball?" Thomas heard William ask Nathan during the bottom of the second. He turned to see how his friend would respond to the question. "Do you enjoy it as much as Sir Thomas?" William added.

He did not answer, but turned, his eyes pleading with Thomas.

Thomas looked back at his notes and continued writing.

"I will tell you about John McGraw," William continued. "You tell me if you've heard any of this, okay? Then tell me anything you know. Okay?"

From his peripheral vision, Thomas saw Nathan turn occasionally. But he continued writing the sequence of McGinnity's pitches, staying focused on the paper on which he wrote.

Philadelphia scored one run in the third.

By the end of six, the Giants had only two hits.

"Heap much, Chief!" The fan behind them grew louder.

"Sometimes," Thomas heard William tell Nathan, "sportswriters call McGraw 'Little Napoleon.' That's funny, don't you think?"

In the eighth inning, the Athletics scored another two runs.

The Giants had two more singles but still had not scored.

The chanting fan had garnered more of a following – the fans apparently hoping that their ridicule would affect Bender's performance.

Drum impersonations and war cries echoed amongst the stands.

When the bottom of the eighth inning began, and the chanting of the fans trying to unnerve Bender increased in derisiveness, in the midst of another bit of trivia that William was narrating, Nathan stood.

Thomas looked at his friend standing in the middle of the aisle. He was taller than any of the players, and though his gut was flabby, his broad shoulders and thick torso commanded respect. Nathan tucked in his shirt and straightened it so the buttons ran down the center. He swiped the left sleeve of his jacket with his right hand, removing the last traces from wiping his nose earlier that morning. He tugged the rim of his hat and with his hands groomed his beard as well as hands could groom a beard.

"Excuse me." He lightly placed his hand atop William's head and shuffled passed Thomas onto the steps that led to the seats above them. With purpose, he slowly walked up the steps to the row where the leader of the chants was seated.

William turned in his seat and followed Nathan's movement. Thomas looked over his shoulder, uncertain what his friend was up to.

"Heap much, Chief Bender!" the chanting fan had just finished shouting.

The fan was on the edge of the row, and Nathan stopped when he reached it. Several seconds passed before the chanting fan realized somebody was standing next to him. At first, the fan shifted in his seat, as if to give room for Nathan to pass. But Nathan did not move.

The man looked up.

Nathan lowered to his knees and leaned toward the fan, whispering into his ear.

The whispered monologue lasted ten, maybe fifteen, maybe twenty seconds. The longer his friend was leaning close to the chanting fan, the more uncomfortable Thomas grew.

When Nathan finished, the fan looked away, then looked down. His shoulders drooped, and his eyes were downcast.

Nathan stood and lightly tapped the young man's shoulder several times before he walked back down the steps to his seat.

"Excuse me," he said as he shuffled passed Thomas and again lightly placed his hand atop William's head.

Thomas could still hear distant chants throughout the stadium, but none near their seats.

Charles Bender surrendered four hits, struck out nine batters, and gave up no runs. The series was tied at one.

While the fans began to leave, Thomas heard his name shouted. "Mr. Kemp!"

He turned and saw a police officer holding a note.

"That's me," Thomas announced.

The officer extended his hand. "A message from Mr. McGraw."

Thomas opened the note immediately:

On the walk to the hotel, Thomas heard Nathan ask William, "So, tell me again why they call McGraw 'Little Napoleon'."

When they checked out of the hotel on Wednesday morning, the clerk handed a package to Thomas. "For Mr. Jennings," he announced.

Thomas handed the package to William, who, upon receiving it, ran to a chair and ripped open the brown wrap. Inside the box was the morning edition of the *New York Times*. Near the top, written over the leading stories about theft, bribery, and the rebuilding of Russia following the war with Japan, was a handwritten note in bold black ink:

"Thanks for the education yesterday. It helped me understand the passage on page eight."

Thomas stood over William, watching him run his fingers through the newspaper until he reached the eighth page.

In the first column, Nathaniel Marsh had underlined the following:

> McGinnity lasted eight innings. In their half of the eighth the Athletics batted in a brace of runs. Napoleon McGraw summoned his marshals, viewed the field of conflict, and decided that it was about time for the Prussians to arrive. He substituted Ames as a forlorn hope, but the day was gone, the Giants had been vanquished.

Rain in Philadelphia forced the Wednesday game to be played on Thursday.

Another note arrived from McGraw on Wednesday afternoon. Thomas knew it was time to take action—he needed to convince McGraw to stop this nonsense.

Thomas had learned of McGraw's competitiveness firsthand at St. Bonaventure. It was an obsession. Whenever Thomas had read stories of McGraw's antics on the field as he coached one of the bases—tripping opposing players or holding the belts of the first or third basemen—none of it surprised him. Whereas his friend and former Orioles teammate,

Hughie Jennings, shared an equal commitment to victory, he pursued it with joy, making friends of opponents, fans, and umpires. McGraw, on the other hand, left enemies in his wake, expecting everyone to implement any tactic to gain a win.

The odd thing was that off the field, in anything that had little or nothing to do with the game, McGraw was a decent guy. He had a big heart. But if a win was at stake, McGraw's "goodness" vanished. He expected everybody to operate under the same gamesmanship as he.

So, when Thomas read McGraw's short notes, they didn't surprise him. Somehow McGraw had learned of Thomas's employment under Ban Johnson—probably via Hughie Jennings. And even though McGraw certainly could not expect a Xaverian Brother to be a mole for the opposing team, still Little Napoleon asked, apparently oblivious to the loss of integrity it would cost Thomas.

Wednesday evening, Thomas decided to play McGraw's game.

It wouldn't be the first time in his life he did something of the sort.

Thomas recalled that when he was a child in grammar school, the class jester raised his head during a math exam and poked his head over Thomas's shoulder to get a glimpse of Thomas's sheet. Thomas took action—he intentionally answered all thirty questions incorrectly, waited for the jester to walk his exam to the front of the class, then erased all thirty answers and completed the exam correctly.

He sat at the desk in his room and wrote to McGraw:

Thomas took some solace in that the note did contain an element of truth. The Athletics hitters were looking for the fastball as long as they were at the plate with less than two strikes. Once Matty had them in the hole, however, their strategy changed to look for the off-speed, but to lay off Matty's fadeaway.

He took further solace in that he was assured that whatever he told McGraw was pointless. Complete vanity. Mathewson looked invincible, regardless of any information the Athletics may have. McGraw had no reason to seek out an insurance policy—he had Matty!

The Giants scored two runs in the first, five runs in the fifth, and another two in the ninth. All but the first run were superfluous since Mathewson shut out the Athletics again. Even with two strikes, Matty was throwing heat. It was as though McGraw didn't get the note. Or that he hadn't shared the knowledge with Matty. Or that Matty didn't care.

The Giants led the series 2–1.

The following day, McGinnity outpitched Eddie Plank, beating the Athletics 1–0.

With the championship in sight, Little Napoleon sent his best of the "imperial guard" to vanquish the enemy. Mathewson shut out the Athletics for the third time in less than a week, besting Charles Bender, the Giants winning the game 2–0 and the series 4–1.

Chapter 6

The first time he noticed it was in Boston three years earlier in the hotel where they stayed, just blocks from the ballpark. When he woke that morning, while Sir Thomas was placing his cassock over his head, William saw the small wooden-framed picture on the stand next to Sir Thomas's bed. He did not recall seeing it the prior evening, but he had been tired and sad after saying goodbye to Timmy just hours earlier. Perhaps he didn't recall seeing it. But when he saw the picture again on the stand next to Thomas's bed at the hotel in Pittsburgh, William realized the picture belonged to Sir Thomas.

He recalled rising from under the covers and walking slowly to the nightstand while Thomas was in the washroom. William knelt beside the picture to get a closer look. A younger version of Sir Thomas was in the far left of the picture. He wasn't wearing his cassock but a pair of dirty suspenders, just like the three men to his right.

"You recognize any of them?" William had turned to see Sir Thomas approach from behind. Sir Thomas picked up the photograph and looked at it with what seemed to William as sadness, similar to the sadness he felt over missing Timmy.

William nodded and pointed to the younger Thomas in the far left of the photograph.

It was then that Thomas had introduced William to the other three men in the picture.

"Perhaps," Thomas had said, smiling, "you will make their acquaintances one day."

Three years had passed and now he held the picture in his outstretched arms, looking down upon it as he sat at Thomas's bedside at the Palmer House Hotel on the shores of Lake Michigan. He looked up from the picture and studied Sir Thomas, who was asleep. He had been sleeping throughout most of the day and on into the evening, waking only when coughing fits convulsed his body. They had arrived in Chicago on Monday with plenty of time to explore the city in which Sir Thomas expressed such pride. He had promised William to escort him to Jackson Park, where he had helped construct the buildings of the world's fair fifteen years earlier alongside his three friends in the picture. He had promised William to treat him to the best pizza on the face of the earth and to take him to the concert hall just blocks from their hotel to hear the renowned violinist Frederik Frederiksen and his wife, English pianist Grace Frederiksen, perform works of Brahms, Rubinstein, and Liszt. And though it was not promised, it was understood that they would attend all the games of the championship series between the crosstown rivals, the Cubs and the White Sox.

On the train eastward, William sensed something was not right. Though Sir Thomas had brought the satchel filled with notepads and listings of scores in the daily paper, not once had he released the latch of the satchel to reach inside and study the National League players.

They attended the first game on Tuesday afternoon to watch the heavily favored Cubs get beaten 2–1 by the hapless Hitless Wonders of the American League. Early in the second inning, William looked over at Sir Thomas. The pen with which he had scribbled a few notes was on the concrete floor of West Side Park. The pad of paper had slipped from Thomas's lap and was nestled between his left leg and the metal handrest that separated the seats. Thomas's head was limp, resting on his left shoulder. He began snoring a few moments later—enough to cause some of the fans near them to turn and look, initially with surprise, then later with annoyance. Spittle dropped from his mouth onto his cassock.

When William shook him, Thomas opened his eyes, then seconds later fell back to sleep.

Fortunately, the game was short. Each team had only four hits. The Cubs ace, Mordecai "Three Finger" Brown, would have easily won the game had his team hit as they normally did. Whereas the White Sox used three of their four hits to score both of their runs, the White Sox pitcher, Nick Altrock, scattered the four hits he surrendered in different innings, leaving the Cubs few scoring opportunities.

When the game was over, William again shook Sir Thomas. His slumber had grown deeper, it seemed. Not until the stands were empty and William resumed the shaking did a police officer come to assist. He woke Sir Thomas, and the shock of seeing a police officer caused enough fright to energize Thomas's walk to the elevated metro station. William asked another officer for help loading Sir Thomas onto the train and for instructions as to which stop to exit. The kindly officer boarded the train with them, exited at the closest stop to the Palmer House, and assisted Thomas through the streets, into the hotel lobby, up the stairs, and onto his bed.

"Thank you, Officer," William offered. "Not sure how I would have got him back."

The officer held out his hand, grabbed William on the elbow, and shook his arm with gentle vigor. "If he is not better, call the lobby, ask to have a doctor look at him."

William nodded.

When William woke the next morning, Thomas was still sleeping. Occasionally he would awaken, endure a coughing spell, and then hold his stomach as though he were in horrible pain.

He received no instructions from Sir Thomas that morning, no indication if he should call a doctor or ask the hotel for assistance or send a telegraph to the other brothers so they could advise him what to do. Uncertain of what steps to take, he saw a calm on Sir Thomas's face as he snored—Thomas even pulled the blanket up under his chin. Perhaps another day's sleep would make him better. And with this hope William left the hotel, walked to the elevated train, spotted a group of baseball fans, and followed them, uncertain how to navigate to South Side Park, the home of the White Sox.

How aptly the sportswriters refer to the Sox as the Hitless Wonders, he thought. The day before, the Sox had four hits. Today the Cubs pitcher, Ed Reulbach, shut them out, giving up only two hits. Six hits in two games, yet the series was tied at one. William had begun to mock the players, joining the Sox fans around him, amazed at the players' undisciplined swings at pitches—fastballs, curves, slow balls, in the zone, out of the zone, it didn't matter. They had a better chance at hitting the ball if they stepped to the plate with their eyes closed than utilizing whatever approach they were currently using.

Back at the hotel, things had worsened. When he woke the following morning, William noticed Thomas's face had whitened to a pale, lifeless color. His arms were covered with light red spots. His cough was growing increasingly harsh. Beads of sweat fell from his temples. The bedsheets were saturated with perspiration.

He feared to leave the room, and after going downstairs to buy a couple pieces of fruit and a piece of bread from a vendor just outside the hotel's front doors, he rushed back to the room and pulled a chair next to Sir Thomas's bedside. He glanced at the picture of Sir Thomas and his friends. Just like in Boston, just like in Pittsburgh, Philadelphia, and New York, Thomas took it with him. At St. Mary's, the picture hung from a nail on the wall just to the left of Sir Thomas's desk. He didn't recall seeing it there prior to their trip to Boston and Pittsburgh, but when they returned, there it was, and now, whenever he entered Sir Thomas's class, he would sit and look at the picture, becoming lost in the stories Sir Thomas had narrated about the world's fair. He imagined what he and Timmy and George and Congo may look like when they reached the ages of the four friends in the photo.

Even after William had decided he did not want to play an instrument, he was welcomed into the music classroom. If he and Congo and George finished their work early at the shirt factory, George and Congo would rush to the ball field to get there before the other boys, but William would wander back into the main building and cautiously open the door to Sir Thomas's class, making sure not to interrupt the rehearsal of the advanced musicians. Once he entered, he would look to the front of the class and make eye contact with Sir Thomas, hoping it was all right for him to enter. A quick nod meant William could enter, and he would walk quietly to the back and find a chair as far from the musicians as possible. There, he would close his eyes, rest his hands on his knees, and listen.

"What do you think of, William?" Sir Thomas had asked one day after the other boys placed their instruments away and left the classroom. "What is it you hear when you sit back there?"

"Each instrument is so different. Each boy is so different," William answered. "Yet somehow, some way, the sounds mix and I hear a melody. It's beautiful. Pretty. I wish I could describe it better. But that's what I think."

Thomas narrowed his eyes. William sensed he needed to explain.

"Most of the times, when I was in the band playing, I didn't think like that. I was so upset at the ugly sounds I heard from myself that I could hear nothing else. I discovered when I stopped playing there was a magic all around me that I had been missing. And now, I can hear it whenever I come back. I close my eyes and I see Napoleon guiding his generals to the rhythm of the music. I see his generals. I see McGraw and Matty and Honus. All those books you read to me at night, the music makes them come to life."

Sir Thomas had nodded and smiled and lowered his head, laughing. "You know," William recalled him saying, "when I see a bow touch the end of a violin's strings and fingers dancing on and off the other end of the same strings, and I hear the music it creates, well . . . yes, I understand what you are talking about."

William reached for the picture and held it. Sir Thomas looked so young and full of energy back then. Now he looked as if he could not lift himself from bed.

He had hardly any nourishment for three days. He had eaten two pieces of toast on the train from Baltimore. At the game he had cracked open three or four peanuts before he fell asleep in his seat. At the hotel, William had set on the nightstand some apples and though he had never seen Sir Thomas eat, eventually the pieces of fruit were gone.

Suddenly, he heard Thomas wake. He had removed the heavy blanket from his chest and raised himself from the pillows, propping himself against the headboard. He still looked fragile and exhausted, but the expression on his face was similar to how he looked when he was instructing the boys at St. Mary's.

"Listen," he struggled to say, then coughed. "The man next to me in the picture, his name is Elias. Lives near here. A bit outside the city."

He reached under his pillow and grabbed a pad of paper he must have placed there between his sleeping and waking. That he could find it surprised William and encouraged him that perhaps Sir Thomas was on the mend. "Listen," he said again. "Find me a pen in the satchel."

William raced to the closet and found a pen in an inner pocket of the bag.

Sir Thomas began writing. "William. I want you to listen carefully." He looked up, gazing directly into William's eyes. "You understand?" he said.

"Yes, Sir Thomas."

"I was hoping to be stronger. Not sure how long or how serious this will be. I want you to do a few things. I'm making a list."

William stared. Finally, he would have some idea of what needed to be done.

"Here," he said, handing the small sheet of paper to William.

Thomas coughed, held his stomach, pushed himself higher, then leaned toward the picture and pointed to Elias. "He's number one on the list. I want you to find him and ask him to help you. He's a good friend. Lives a few miles to the west. On Tripp Avenue. I wrote the address for you."

William glanced down at the paper: "1249 Tripp Avenue," it read.

"Take the elevated train to the west end of the city. Take the picture with you. Find him. He will help you get back to St. Mary's."

The whole effort exhausted Thomas. His torso dropped back onto the bed.

William read the other two items on the list. The second read, "Contact BJ. At the Drake." That's all it said. No hints as to what to say or do. The third had a large star drawn next to it. "Go to concert tonight. Tickets in satchel. Want full report of violin solos."

William touched the part of the picture in which the younger version of Thomas appeared. He touched it softly and ran his fingers across the top of his head, as if he were the parent and Thomas were the child. He placed the photo back onto the nightstand. He moved the chair closer to Thomas's bedside and leaned close to Thomas's head.

"I will ask the hotel to call for a doctor," William said softly. "Is that okay, Sir Thomas?"

Sir Thomas opened his eyes with great effort. He nodded. "Please."

About two hours later the doctor arrived. As he examined Sir Thomas, William waited in a chair in the corner of the room, watching each move of the doctor, each expression, each instrument he pulled from his bag. Nothing the doctor did indicated the illness was serious.

"Son," the doctor said, still with no expression to tell of the illness's nature. "Come with me into the hallway."

The doctor opened the door, waited for William to leave the room, placed the latch on the doorframe to keep the door from shutting, and knelt down, speaking with William eye to eye.

"How long has he been like this?"

William thought of when he first noticed Sir Thomas not acting like Sir Thomas. "Sunday, maybe Saturday."

The doctor nodded, as if this confirmed something.

"He will need to be taken to a hospital. In isolation. You understand what this means?"

"Isolation?" William repeated.

The doctor nodded.

"Alone. By himself?"

"For now. I think you are fine. I want you to go with us to the hospital. I can test you tonight. As long as you have not eaten any food he's prepared, and he hasn't spit or coughed on you, then you should be fine."

William nodded. Then he nodded with more certainty. Thomas had never prepared a meal for him. Not even cut his pancakes. And why would this make a difference?

"Good," the doctor said with relief. "Now, I'm going to the hotel lobby. You cannot remain in this room. I will ask them to assign another room for you."

Again, William nodded.

The doctor continued. "I want you to stay with us at the hospital tonight. To keep you close. To make sure you are fine and to help us with any more information we need."

"Yes, sir."

"I need to make arrangements with the clerk downstairs and inform them of this room," he said, pointing inside. "I want you to pack a few things in a bag. Touch as little as you have to. Sit in that chair, and wait for me to return."

"Yes, sir."

While William waited, after he had packed some undergarments and socks, he sat in the chair to obediently wait for the doctor's return. As he sat, he noticed Sir Thomas's satchel in the closet. In it would be the tickets for that evening's concert. He ran to it, unlatched it, and fingered through the scant notes Thomas had made. William looked over his shoulder, not wanting to be seen touching the bag belonging to someone so gravely ill. In the inner pocket of the satchel he found the tickets to the remaining games. As he thumbed through them, he found the concert tickets. He stuffed all the tickets into his pants pocket.

He continued looking through the bag and found a card with the name of the hotel where BJ was staying in Chicago—the Drake. He placed the card in his pocket, then continued searching in case he may find anything else that could be useful. Next, he found some postcards that had information written on them, all addressed to BJ. One said in bold writing at the top, "Game 1," another said "Game 2," and there was one for every game through game seven. Except for the game numbers, the rest of the writing on each card was identical: "Observations," "Focus," and "Recommendations." William placed the seven postcards into the same pocket as the card with BJ's address. He looked over his shoulder, sensing that the doctor was about to return any second. He turned the satchel upside down, and all the contents fell to the floor. William noticed seven small white envelopes, slightly larger than the seven postcards, each envelope addressed to BJ at the Drake. William gathered the seven envelopes and placed them in his pocket.

He looked over his shoulder. Still no doctor. As he stuffed the other papers back into Sir Thomas's satchel, he saw on the nightstand the Tuesday edition of the *Chicago Tribune* he had purchased from the street vendor outside the hotel. He would keep that also.

He secured the latch and set the satchel back into the closet, then returned to his chair and read the front-page cartoon from the previous day's newspaper.

It was entitled "On the Eve of the Great Baseball Contest." It was divided into four scenes, running top to bottom. All scenes included two characters—an elderly office manager dressed in a black coat and business shirt, and a young office boy dressed in knickers and a casual jacket.

In the first slide the manager proclaims, "Young man, I want you to do something for me this afternoon!"

To which the boy replies in the second slide, "I think I have a bad tooth—I mean stomachache."

The manager is relentless and continues. "It's very important, and it will take all afternoon."

The boy responds, "I must have ate something that wasn't agreeable."

The manager persists. "If you don't do it I'll discharge you."

The boy confesses, "I want to go—"

But the old man interrupts. "I want you to go to the ball game with me and explain the fine points of the plays to me."

At which point the young employee is unable to speak coherently and is smiling and clearly no longer suffering from any ailment.

William let the paper rest on his knees. He observed Thomas awaken and struggle to sit up, coughing incessantly until his eyes watered. Blood started to trickle from his nose. The coughing stopped long enough for Thomas to wipe the mucus onto his sleeve. He looked down, noticed the blood, looked over at William, and fell back onto his pillow.

The roles had been reversed from the scene portrayed in the cartoon. The boy had been feigning. Sir Thomas was not.

William heard several voices approaching in the corridor. He jumped from his chair and cracked open the door, peered down the hall, and saw the doctor, a hotel employee, and several nurses walking quickly toward the room. William looked behind at Thomas and immediately rushed to the picture on the bedstand. He picked it up and turned, uncertain where to place it—it was too large to place in his pocket. He turned toward the closet and looked down at the satchel. He looked up at the door. They were just outside. He raced to the closet, grabbed the satchel, placed the picture inside, and rushed back to the chair in which he was to be waiting. He emptied his clothes from his bag and stuffed them inside the satchel. He closed the latch and raised the satchel up, bracing it between his folded arms and chest.

The group of adults entered. Their looks were compassionate, with no hint of suspicion.

"Follow me, sweetie," the prettier of the nurses instructed.

William stood, glanced at Thomas, and followed the pretty nurse into the hall.

When they arrived at the hospital, it seemed everyone was dressed in white. William thought it was a place full of death and fright. Some of the older boys at St. Mary's often teased the younger kids about the nightmarish tales they read in Dante's *Inferno*. The pictures it created in William's mind were often the settings of his scariest dreams. Now, seeing this place where they had taken Sir Thomas left him feeling that the hospital corridors were one of Dante's circles—one step further from life, one step closer to whatever occurred after life.

The doctor asked him a series of questions, most of which he was unable to answer. "Had Brother Kemp been to New York?"

"Yes," William answered.

"Has he been to Long Island?"

William lifted his hands. "I don't know."

"Has he been to Oyster Bay? How long ago was he in New York? Has he ever been ill like this in the past?"

William looked at the doctor, uncertain what the consequences may be for his inability to answer. He saw the doctor's eyes focus on the satchel on the floor, leaning against William's legs.

"Excuse me." The doctor stood and walked several yards away to speak with the pretty nurse.

Now the nurse fixed her eyes on the satchel.

The doctor motioned her to follow him into an office further down the hall.

William jumped from his chair, gripping tightly the satchel in his left hand. He rushed to the window looking into the room in which Sir Thomas was isolated. He placed his hand on the glass, contemplating what he might do. Lowering his head he muttered, "I'm sorry, Sir Thomas," turned and raced to the stairwell, down the steps, into the lobby, and out the hospital's front entrance. He looked up to the second floor, lifted his hand, and waved. "Goodbye, Sir Thomas."

The room in which the doctor had placed Sir Thomas overlooked West Side Park. In the distance, not far from the park, William had recognized the elevated metro stop to which the police officer had walked William and Sir Thomas after the end of the first game. He recalled it was named *Ogden*. He had hoped to see it immediately after leaving the hospital. Now, racing down the street, afraid that one of the hospital employees may be just behind him, he looked up at each building he passed, not wanting to miss the station. "Ogden," William muttered as he continued running around the perimeter of the Cubs' home field. Afraid that he was running in a large circle, he was about to panic when he recognized the buildings of Cook County Hospital just two blocks in front of him. And then he saw it—a large wooden sign with bold black letters that spelled *OGDEN*, with chains attached to both ends of the placard swinging above a stairwell. He turned and jumped two steps with each stride until he reached the platform just in time to catch the train going west.

Fortunately, the car he entered was not crowded. He sat on the corner bench, reached inside the satchel, and studied the picture. He wanted to make sure he would recognize Sir Thomas's friend when he saw him. As he studied the face of Elias, he realized he had met one of the other men in the photo. How had he not recognized him previously? Thomas was on the left, and on the right was the odd man William had met in New York one year earlier. He was clean shaven, with no wild hair.

Just moments earlier he had felt regret and guilt that perhaps he should not have left the hospital. Even now he was not sure what he was running from and wondered what may happen to Sir Thomas. But, realizing he had met two of the four men in Sir Thomas's picture and was on the verge of meeting a third, he felt a thrill he had previously felt only on the ball field. He placed the picture back in the satchel and raised himself in his seat, looking out the window, feeling lost but hopeful.

A train conductor entered his car. "Tripp," the conductor shouted. "Tripp Avenue is the next stop."

Once he exited the train, the walk from the platform to the street was a few short steps. He turned right from Twelfth Street and walked north on Tripp for over an hour. William began to worry, fearing he was walking in the wrong direction. To ask someone for help may raise suspicions as to why a nine-year-old boy was wandering the streets alone. He kept walking another twenty minutes, each step adding anxiety. When he saw a young girl with her mother, he told the mother the address and inquired whether he was walking in the correct direction.

"Yes," the mother replied, with no hint of curiosity. "It's about a mile ahead."

After the mother and daughter passed, William sighed and lowered his head, relieved to learn that he was closer, but frustrated that he was still so far from the home of Sir Thomas's friend.

William hung the strap of the satchel over his shoulder and started to run at a slow pace. He thought of the running drills the brothers required of the boys on the ball field. With each intersection he left behind, he was grateful for the drills and was surprised he had no urge to stop.

Finally, he reached a block where the corner house was number 1231. On the next block, the first house was numbered 1241. He stopped. He reached in his pocket and looked at the address Sir Thomas had written. The first three numbers were the same. He smiled. "One two four nine," he said softly.

In the distance, a group of boys was shouting and cheering. He looked away from the homes and saw the boys scattered at the end of the next block, wearing caps and holding gloves. It looked as if they were playing a form of baseball using a rubber ball that was bouncing high off the pavement while two boys were racing around makeshift bases of wood and cloth. For a moment William felt homesick for St. Mary's, but as he passed the next white picket fence, he looked at the number next to the home's front door. "One two four seven," he read softly.

He stopped in front of the next house and whispered with triumph, "One two four nine."

The beat of his heart surged. He unstrapped the satchel from his shoulder and removed the picture, studying the facial features of Elias. He walked up the steps to the porch, shuffled to the front door, and knocked.

Nobody answered.

He waited about thirty seconds and knocked again.

No answer.

He bit his lower lip, looked behind at the group of boys playing ball, then inched forward, shielded his eyes, and pressed his face against the front door window.

The home was desolate—no furniture, no sign that anybody lived within its walls.

"Ducky!" a voice from behind shouted. "Hey, Ducky!"

William stepped away from the window and turned. At the curb, standing next to the tree between the house of Elias and the next home, was a boy about his height wearing a dirty white cap. He was swinging his arm, brushing his worn glove across his right leg, back and forth, back and forth, as though he were cleaning his grass-stained pants.

"Hey, Ducky," the boy continued. "What you doing up there?"

The boy's chin was raised. He was smiling and seemed to be waiting for an answer. The other boys were shouting, growing impatient, wanting to continue their game, William assumed. It seemed that the group of boys were all beckoning their friend, but the boys were using numerous names when addressing him.

"Merlin!" several of the boys were shouting. "Take your position!"

Others were yelling, "Buck! Hurry up! What you doing over there?"

Others were calling out, "Jonesy!" and "Merl!"

The boy ignored the calls. He stepped over the curb and onto the lawn under the tree.

He had a kind face. Suddenly, his smile disappeared. Just seconds earlier the boy at the curb appeared amused by William's presence on the porch, but now he looked worried, like one of the brothers might appear when students in their class were having problems grasping the material they were teaching.

William looked past him, alarmed as the other boys began walking in their direction. He would ask why they were not at school on a Thursday in the middle of October, but they may ask the same of him. They were a mixed group. About half of them looked light skinned like him. Most of the others, like Merlin, had charcoal skin, just as a couple of the boys at St. Mary's did. Sir Thomas once told him that the darker boys were no different than he was, they were orphans just like he was, only their grandparents were likely to have been slaves. "Slaves," William recalled thinking, "Slavery meant Civil War, and Civil War meant photographs taken by Matthew Brady," and that set his imagination on fire, thinking of the lessons learned in history class. The group got closer as the boy approached the steps of the home.

"Hey, Ducky," he said once more. "Are you okay?"

William walked toward him, shaking his head side to side. "Do you know the family that lives here?"

"Nobody lives there, Ducky," the boy answered. "Moved about two months ago. Somewhere in Missouri, I think."

The hope he felt moments earlier left all at once. William handed the picture to the boy, pointing at Elias.

"That's him!" the boy declared. "My dad says he built a lot of homes in the neighborhood!"

With each new piece of information, William felt an increasing dread. He dropped to the top step and sat, feeling lost. What was he to do now? How was he to get back to St. Mary's?

He felt the sun warming his face until the boy stood a few feet from him, blocking the sun's rays. "I'm Merlin," he said, extending his hand. "Some of the boys call me Merl for short. Or Jonesy 'cause my last name is Jones. Some call me Buck, which is short for Bucket, 'cause they say I catch any ball hit in my vicinity. Normally, I think up the names in the neighborhood, but you can't come up with your own nickname, right?"

William agreed by nodding.

"I call you Ducky," Merlin continued, " 'cause I saw you flyin' down the street 'til you reached us here. Y'know ducks can fly? Just like they can run and swim. You looked pretty fast, but you were wobbling back and forth, guess 'cause you carrying that bag over your shoulder. Kinda reminded me of a duck, is all. Hope you don't mind."

The boy's stream of dialogue provided a momentary diversion from the predicament William felt enveloping him. He looked up and offered a constrained grin. "I need to get back to the city."

"Really!" Merlin said, almost in a shout. "I need to meet my dad there. Probably running a little late, I am."

Merlin looked back at the group of boys several feet away, still in the street. "Game's over, gang," he announced. "Got to go meet Pops."

It took less than a minute for the boys to disperse, setting off at different paces in all directions, shouting their farewells to one another.

"You play ball?" Merlin asked.

"Sure."

"You any good?"

"I pitch better than I hit. I field better than I pitch."

Merlin smiled. "All right, Ducky! I like that! Not too high on yourself, eh?"

William shrugged.

"Tell you what, Duck," Merlin said as he stepped from the vacant home, jumped off the curb, and landed in the middle of the street. "I'm running late. Have to help Pops sell nuts outside the game today. Where you headed?"

"You're going to the game?" William stood, his eyes wide, feeling a bolt of hope.

"The game? No," Merlin answered, "but I'll be outside the ballpark. Pops has a stand 'cross the north entrance. Usually sells out since the crowd's so big."

"That's where I need to go. Can I follow you?"

"Sure 'nough, Ducky!"

William stopped. Merlin was walking in the wrong direction, away from the station where William arrived two hours earlier. "But the Tripp station is this way!" he said.

Merlin turned, covering his mouth with his right hand, laughing. "You ran all that way?"

"Yes."

"That be 'bout five miles, Ducky!"

William looked southward over his shoulder, as far as he could see. "Really?"

"Follow me," Merlin invited. "Logan Square jus' 'round the corner."

When they arrived at the north entrance of West Side Park, Merlin ran to a wooden pushcart, opened one of its swinging doors, and began filling a large cloth bag with peanuts and small paper bags.

"Pops!" Merlin shouted at a balding middle-aged man, about the same age as Sir Thomas. "Which gate you want me at?"

"Who's your friend, son?" the man asked.

Merlin continued filling the bag with peanuts using his left hand and invited William to step closer by beckoning him with the right. "Ducky," he said, "this is Pops."

Still filling the bag, he turned his attention to his father. "Pops, this is Ducky."

The man's face was kind, just like his son's. He smiled and chuckled a bit. "Ducky," he said, almost apologetically, "you have a real name?"

"William, sir."

Pops extended his hand. "Nice to meet you, William."

"Well," Merlin announced, "I'm off to sell some nuts!"

"Wait a minute!" William shouted.

His outburst shocked himself and appeared to stun Merlin and his father as well as Pop's customers.

He had an idea and was calculating how to say what he was thinking.

"Merlin," he started. "You were telling me on the train that your Pop has been selling out 'cause of the large crowds and that with warmer weather today, even larger crowds may show up—right?"

"Sure," Merlin answered.

"And that your Pop has even more nuts to sell today, and that he's not sure if he will be able to sell them all, right?"

"Yeah?"

"What if we could sell them inside?"

Merlin and his father and the customers were looking at William as though he were speaking nonsense.

"Inside the park?" Merlin repeated. "You want to sell the nuts inside the park, at the game?"

"Yes!" William answered.

Merlin stepped closer to William. He tugged his hat snug over his eyes. "Ducky," he said with a hint of condescension, "How are we getting inside? Even if Pop could afford to buy a ticket—"

"William," Pop said as he handed some change to a customer, "the game is sold out. There are no—"

William reached into his pocket and pulled out the two tickets for game three. "How about these!" he exclaimed, holding them up to Pop.

Within two minutes, Pop confirmed with a customer that the tickets were valid, pulled another cloth bag from his cart, loaded it full of nuts, and placed it over William's shoulder.

"Five cents a bag," he instructed William. "Fill the bags with nuts, sell each bag for five cents. You're good at math?"

"Yes, sir," William answered.

"Godspeed to you both," Pop said as he rubbed his hands together, smiling while he made another sale. "Godspeed to Merlin," William heard Pop chant. "Godspeed to Ducky!"

The plan was to make circuits around the inside of the stadium until there were no more nuts. By the time they met in the outfield bleachers, almost behind Solly Hofman, the Cubs center fielder, each boy's bag was empty. William looked at the large clock on the building across the street. It was 2:23.

"We've seven minutes," he said to Merlin. "Follow me!"

By the time Jack Pfiester made his first pitch, the boys were seated. It looked promising for the Cubs in the first, getting two hits off "Big Ed" Walsh. But at the end of five, Walsh had struck out six and had allowed only one more Cub to reach base, walking Frank Chance with two out in the fourth. The White Sox were living up to their reputation, having only three hits. At the end of five it was 0–0.

"They have no discipline," William whispered to Merlin. "Look at them. What have they done today? Struck out seven times! And it's only the fifth inning."

"They're lucky," Merlin replied. "The Sox are lucky the league allows Walsh to throw that spitball of his. Ain't no way the Cubs could be held back if it weren't for that spitter!"

Merlin stood, turned around, and began waving as if he were beckoning someone. William turned and saw a police officer walking down the aisle in their direction. It was the same officer who helped lead Sir Thomas from his seat two days earlier.

"What is it, boys?" the officer asked, kneeling. "How can I help you?"

Merlin was still standing. He pointed toward the pitcher's mound. "You have a citation book with you, Officer?" Merlin shouted, like he was one of the older boys at St. Mary's, performing in a school play.

The officer reached inside his coat and held it out toward Merlin.

"That man out there," Merlin said as he pointed behind him at Ed Walsh, "he's putting what ought to be an illegal substance on the ball, giving unfair advantage to his team. Ain't much likelihood that Solly, Sheckard, Schulte, Tinker, Evers, and Chance be stymied if he weren't cheating out there. Can't you write him up a ticket?"

The officer smiled, and fans near them started laughing and clapping, some saying, "That's right!"

Some yelled, "Preach it, little man!"

Others chanted, "Write him up! Write him up! Write up the spitballer!"

Earlier, when the boys entered the park and raced to their seats, William observed isolated fans looking with anger at Merlin. Several fans seemed to intentionally walk toward him and shove him. Some even shouted, "What are you doing here?" or "Who let you in?" William concluded it must be the color of Merlin's skin, since there were no other fans at the game that looked like Merlin. But the fans seated around them did not seem to mind—they seemed happy Merlin was there, laughing with him and following his lead.

The officer laid his hand softly on William's shoulder and bent in close, asking, "How's your friend from the other day?"

William looked up and felt like he wanted to cry. The officer cared about Sir Thomas, a man he had met only once. Yet here was William, enjoying a ball game, laughing with his new friend, while he ought to be across the street seeking some way to help Sir Thomas get better.

William frowned. "Not well."

Other fans near them, ones he recognized from two days earlier, asked William about Sir Thomas also. They must have noticed how he slept through the game. William had never before felt that he was the center of attention—never felt so many people, so many strangers, show genuine concern. Even Merlin had ceased with his antics and was quiet, looking strangely at William, wearing that look of concern William had observed earlier in the day while he stood on the porch of Elias's former home. All the concern from these people filled him with a warmth he had never felt, but this warmth was battling the growing burden of guilt he felt for running from the hospital that morning, deserting the man who had shown him the most kindness of anyone in his life.

Walsh ended the game with twelve strikeouts, surrendering only the two first-inning hits. The White Sox won the game 3–0, taking a series lead of 2–1.

The weather was getting warmer. Tomorrow was Friday, guaranteeing even larger crowds over the weekend. Pop invited William to stay at their home when Merlin divulged the information he had gathered from the officer and the fans. When William told Pop the full story, Pop insisted he stay with their family until he found a way back to St. Mary's.

"God is watching over you, son," Pop declared, after he learned that Sir Thomas was at Cook County Hospital. "My wife cleans the rooms on the colored floors—but I will ask her to get word on your friend. We'll see what we can do."

"Thank you, Mr. Jones," William responded, "but we were going to a concert tonight. I promised him that I'd go and tell him all about it. I need to stay at the hospital."

Merlin's father looked confused, like he was attempting to solve a math problem.

"Can Merlin go with you?" he asked.

"A concert?" Merlin shouted out. "Me?"

"Yes, sir," William answered. "I have two tickets."

And so, Pop used most of his profit that day to purchase a new suit for his son. He and his wife went to a café near Music Hall and waited while the boys attended the concert.

William was a bit fearful that the ushers may not allow two boys to enter without adult supervision, and with the looks Merlin received from some of the fans at the game earlier, he wondered whether Merlin's skin color might be a problem. But when they approached the entrance, a large group of schoolchildren about the same age as William and Merlin were handing their tickets to an usher. The two boys mixed with the twenty or thirty other children and entered just after them.

"You ever been to one of these?" Merlin whispered once they had been seated.

"No," William answered. "You?"

Merlin grinned, shaking his head. "Uh-uh."

The boys each held the program they received upon entering the concert hall. It was a single sheet of heavy paper and read:

Concert at Music Hall

Thursday, October 11, 1906, 8:15 p.m.

Mr. Frederik Frederiksen – Violin

Mrs. Grace Frederiksen – Piano

I. Violin – Piano Duets:

- Sonata in D Minor, opus 108   Johannes Brahms-Germany
- Sonata in E Minor   Emil Sjögren- Sweden

II. Piano Solos:

- G Minor Barcarolle & Valse Caprice   A. Rubinstein- Russia
- Hungarian Rhapsody no. 2   Franz Liszt- Aust-Hungary

III. Violin Solos:

- Rhapsody Suedoise   Emile Sauret- France
- Andante et Allegro Vivace   Niccolo Paganini- Italy arranged by Emile Sauret
- Gavotte and Musette   Tor Aulin- Sweden
- Mazurka no. 2   Felix Borowski- Poland/Eng.

William determined to use the program like the evaluation sheets he created for ballplayers and historical figures. He turned the sheet over, opened the fountain pen, and drew a large *T*.

"Look at that!" Merlin gasped, pointing at the program. "Just imagine—from all these different countries, and . . . and . . . now we get to hear their music!"

"Uh-huh," William muttered. He was feeling a bit overwhelmed with the assignment Sir Thomas had given him. How was he to summarize in words the music he was about to hear?

From the time he and Merlin entered, there was a constant hum of conversation. Men and women were dressed in the finest clothing, nodding and smiling, looking excited, their faces expressing what William felt whenever he entered any of the ballparks he visited with Sir Thomas. There was a seriousness about the place, but also a lightness, as if all the adults around them were children again.

A few minutes after they were seated, a man came out onto the small stage several yards from their seats. He was dressed in black and white. His black shoes shone. He held a violin in one hand, a bow in the other. Light applause scattered across the auditorium, its volume rising. Then it crescendoed to a thunder when a woman in a flowing, sparkling black gown joined the man. The man transferred the bow to the same hand holding the violin, then reached across to the woman and held her hand as they bowed slowly to the crowd.

They released their hands, and the woman walked gracefully to the piano, just to the right of center stage. She swung her right arm behind, gathered the flowing fabric of her gown, and slowly sat on the bench.

From the first note of Brahms's sonata, as Mr. Frederiksen's right arm guided the bow downward, creating what William felt was a crying note so beautiful he could almost weep, something surged within William's chest. With each bow movement, William grew more spellbound. Although Mr. Frederiksen's eyes were shut, his facial expressions constantly changed as the sonata progressed. The melody was enchanting by itself, but when William observed Mr. Frederiksen's left hand wobble or tremble or do whatever it was doing to accentuate the sounds created with the bow, the surge William felt within increased. He looked next to him. Merlin also seemed entranced, his eyes wide, his mouth open. William inched forward in his seat, feeling an anticipation he hadn't felt even at a ball game.

For a short moment, the piano took over the melody and Mr. Frederiksen rested. William glanced toward Mrs. Frederiksen and grew fascinated with her beauty. Her fingers moved with grace, her body swayed to the left, then to the right, following the direction of her hands across the keys. At other times she leaned forward, then back, keeping time with the tempo of the melody. As Mr. Frederiksen began playing once more, William looked back at him. Yet his attention flitted back toward Mrs. Frederiksen. Her regal grace and confident fingers were every bit as entrancing as the skills of her husband.

Then William did what he usually did whenever he entered Sir Thomas's classroom: he leaned back, set his hands on his knees, and closed his eyes. He imagined a woman walking him to school, cooking him dinner, tucking the sheets tightly under his mattress, and bending over to kiss him on the top of his head. Her face resembled Mrs. Frederiksen's. He imagined a home where he played with a cat and dog in a large room with a shiny wooden floor. He imagined a bedroom next to a large room with shelves filled with books. He imagined a man reading in a large chair next to a fireplace. His face resembled Sir Thomas's.

He had once asked Sir Thomas what his favorite instrument was, thinking he would say a piano or organ since that is what William heard him play the day they met. But Sir Thomas had said it was a violin. "The deep melody created by strings that cry," he had said, "wraps me with a beauty and sadness that I don't believe any words could ever express." William was not sure what he meant at the time, but he felt he was beginning to understand.

William opened his eyes. The peaceful piano melody joined with the intensity of Mr. Frederiksen's violin. He too was swaying, like his wife, but each movement he made, each expression on his face, each eyebrow rising and ebbing seemed to be saying to William, "Do you understand now?"

William lowered his head toward the program on which he had written nothing. "No," he answered softly. "I understand nothing."

As the night progressed, William was more conscientious. Next to Sjögren's sonata he wrote, "repetitive, climbing melody. At times could put me to sleep, then a high-pitched screech along with pounding piano would wake me."

And next to Rubinstein's barcarolle: "Fast, fun, lively. Imagine skipping through fields of St. Mary's." Liszt's "Hungarian Rhapsody" heightened William's playfulness: "feel like dancing. So fast and quick, it would be perfect to play while Brother Mathias is hitting fly ball after fly ball to us." The remaining scores were more of the same, William writing words and phrases such as *fun, smiling, Christmas-like, speedy, hopping, couldn't stop tapping my foot, bow hopping off strings, makes me feel like a leprechaun.*

Once the Frederiksens played the final note of Borowski's mazurka, the audience rose to their feet and applauded. Still seated, William and Merlin looked at one another and jumped to their feet.

"One day," Merlin said that evening as the boys lay in bed side by side in Merlin's bedroom, "one day, Ducky, you and I . . . one day the two of us will go to all those places where that music was written. Wouldn't that be something?"

"Uh-huh," William answered, feeling ashamed he hadn't captured in words anything that would help Sir Thomas understand what he had witnessed that evening.

At South Side Park the next day, Mordecai Brown shut out the Sox on two hits. The Cubs scored one run in the seventh, evening the series at two. Again, the boys sold out of peanuts. And when Merlin's mother returned home that evening, she informed William that his friend was still sleeping. No improvement.

Two things kept running through William's mind, preventing him from falling asleep: what to do about Sir Thomas, and what, if anything, could be done to improve the dismal batting lineup of the White Sox. Yes, the series was even, but in the four games the Sox had a total of twelve hits. "That's just three hits each game!" William kept repeating to himself in bed. "Three hits!"

And so, to occupy the early morning hours while Merlin and his parents were sleeping, William got out from under the covers, reached inside the satchel, and took out a pen and the card addressed to BJ for game number five.

He knew that the words he chose would have to be just right. There was a chance that he could get in trouble. But the potential result was worth the risk. The card was small, so he needed to be brief:

William asked Merlin for directions to the Drake Hotel. "I need to leave a note there for one of Sir Thomas's friends."

They took the elevated train to the shore of Lake Michigan, and William entered the lobby of the Drake, leaving the note he had written. Then the two boys boarded the train south for the next game at West Side Park. They sold out of peanuts and watched Walsh win his second game in three days. The Cubs, however, hit much better, scoring six runs in the first six innings. The Sox uncharacteristically had twelve hits and scored eight runs. The lineup was led by the second baseman, Frank Isbell, who hit doubles in four consecutive plate appearances, and the cleanup hitter, shortstop George Davis, who hit two doubles, scored two runs, and hit in three of the eight runs.

The Sox were leading the series 3–2, and on their way back to Merlin's home, William was constructing in his mind the contents of the letter he would leave at the Drake Hotel the next morning:

Dear Mr. Johnson,

Happy to see Sox hit – hope they keep hitting. Brown's curve missed plate during late innings of game 4. Still, the Sox swing and got only two hits. Why not let curves pass without swinging? If we lucky, maybe Brown can't throw curve over plate next game. Sit on fastball and swing if straight.

William (For BTK)

The first five games had all been won by the visiting team. So when Solly Hofman led the game off for the visiting Cubs with a single and scored two batters later, that trend seemed to continue. But the Sox had two singles and two doubles in the first inning, scoring three runs. In the second, they scored four runs on five hits. In less than two innings, the Hitless Wonders had scored seven runs off one of the most highly regarded pitchers in the National League. The final score was 8–3, and the Sox won the series four games to two.

William wanted to jump onto the field with the thousands of fans at South Side Park. He had contributed to their victory, albeit in an underhanded way. He had written the notes with the hope that BJ would conclude William had only written the words that Sir Thomas had dictated to him. That was not the case. And if BJ had ever learned the truth, William was certain he'd be in trouble.

It appeared the Sox had utilized the information on the cards, and he felt proud and excited that he may have contributed to the Sox victory. he felt a nagging, nudging, discomfort that his intention to mislead BJ had been successful.

The boys had once more sold all the peanuts in their bags, contributing to great financial gain for Pop. The three of them traveled north on the train to Grand Central, then waited for the westbound train to take them close to Merlin and Pop's home.

As they were about to board, William heard a voice from behind shouting. "Pops! Don't board!"

William turned and saw Merlin's mother racing toward them. When she reached them, she stopped, out of breath, bent over, hands on her knees.

"It's time," she struggled to say.

"Damn!" Pop responded.

Merlin placed his hand on William's shoulder and squeezed.

"Ducky," Mrs. Jones began, "Brother Thomas is not well. His breathing has grown irregular."

Whatever he felt when he and Timmy were separated three years earlier, whatever sadness that was, it was stronger this time.

"Follow me," Mrs. Jones invited.

The four of them hurried several blocks to the entrance of the hospital. Though Mrs. Jones had been out of breath, she lead the way, causing William to imagine that perhaps she was the source of Merlin's athletic prowess.

Merlin's mother spoke with a receptionist. The receptionist rose from her seat behind the desk, grabbed William's hand, and raced with him upstairs.

When they arrived on the second floor, William recognized the window where he had said goodbye four days earlier. To his left he heard a familiar voice—Brother Mathias was speaking with a doctor and several people he did not recognize. Brother Mathias embraced an elderly woman who was weeping. An elderly man was several feet away, his head bowed, his hands held in a small circle with two younger women and two young men.

"That is his family, sweetie," the nurse informed William.

He looked inside Thomas's room. There were children not much older than William speaking with Sir Thomas, though Thomas's eyes were shut and William figured he was not aware of his surroundings.

William looked from the children to the group of adults and saw Brother Mathias's eyes turn to look at him. William lowered his head and shook it, unwilling to accept the reality of what was happening.

"William." Brother Mathias approached with outstretched arms. He knelt before William and embraced him. The warmth from Mathias's cassock was a temporary haven.

"William," Mathias continued, "come. Follow me. I want you to meet Brother Thomas's family. His parents and siblings."

He looked up. The old man and woman. The younger women and men. The children in the room with Sir Thomas. These were his parents, his brothers and sisters, his nieces and nephews. Sir Thomas had a family? It was a thought that had never entered William's mind.

The thoughts and emotions and confusion and sounds surrounding him were overwhelming enough. But when he saw BJ emerge from the stairwell, face reddening as he walked briskly toward William, all William could do was raise his arms and cover his face.

"Ban Johnson?" he heard Brother Mathias mutter in awe.

"Where is Thomas Kemp?" BJ shouted to the nurses.

William was relieved when he saw how Mathias towered over BJ in height. Mathias placed his hands down upon BJ's shoulders and guided him toward the glass window looking into Thomas's room.

"Children," Mathias called, "let this man speak with his friend."

The children obediently walked from the room as BJ approached Thomas's bedside and pulled a handkerchief from his coat pocket. He removed his spectacles and wiped his eyes. Then he held Thomas's right hand tightly between his hands.

Five minutes passed. Mathias walked to the door with William and knocked, startling BJ. BJ walked to William, knelt, and wrapped his arms around him. "Whatever happened these last two days," he said softly to William, "whatever you were thinking—leading me to believe the words written were from Thomas—in the end, it worked. And as angry as I was this afternoon, when I learned of Thomas's condition, I'd be remiss if I didn't say thank you."

BJ released William from his embrace, rose from his knees, reached down, and lifted William off the floor. "He loved you so much," BJ whispered through tears.

BJ lowered William back down, left the room, and went to speak with Thomas's family.

Mathias prodded William closer to Sir Thomas's side.

"Speak to him," Mathias encouraged. "Let him hear your voice."

William did not know what to say, so he did what he remembered BJ had done. He picked up Sir Thomas's hand and sandwiched it between his hands.

"You were right about the Sox," he said. "They are not very good at batting. Somehow they won two of the first four games, then they started hitting like we all thought the Cubs would hit. It ended today. The Hitless Wonders are champs."

William looked behind him, unsure if it was appropriate to be talking baseball in such circumstances. Mathias grinned and nodded.

"I was thinking what you said 'bout the Cubs—how good they are, how many games they won, winning almost eight of every ten games. Maybe Frank Chance and the whole team think it easy to defeat the Sox. Maybe . . . maybe that's why the Cubs didn't play so well. Like you told me 'bout Napoleon marching into Russia—thought he was invincible . . . "

Again, William looked back at Brother Mathias. This gentle giant whom he and all the boys of St. Mary's revered and respected and yearned to please was looking at William with an expression that resembled the looks he often saw from Thomas when they discussed books.

William released Thomas's hand and reached down to pick up the satchel he had set at the base of the chair when he entered the room. He opened it and took out some papers. "I've been doing what you told me," he said, "watching for strengths, looking for weakness, keeping lists of key players . . . to see if they learn, if they adjust. Look!" William held out a page full of writing. "It's Johnny Evers. I noticed he has trouble with curves. But next time he faces that same pitcher, if that pitcher throws the curve again, Evers will smack it hard—usually for a hit."

Sir Thomas lay still, the heavy sheet on his chest rising every several seconds—the only indication there was still hope he would emerge. William placed the papers back in the satchel and wrapped his hands around Sir Thomas's right hand. He inched forward in his chair and leaned in closer, thinking perhaps this may help Thomas hear him.

"I went to the concert on Thursday. You would have . . . it was—how did you say it? Crying strings? That's how he played the violin. He made the strings cry."

As he spoke each word, he became increasingly aware that he was speaking with Sir Thomas for the last time. He would never see him again.

"Why are the strings so sad, Sir Thomas?" William whispered.

He lowered his head until it rested on the side of Thomas's chest.

"How can the music they create be so sad and yet sound so pretty?"

For Further Reading

Game events described in the narrative are based on the summaries and box scores from accounts appearing in the main editions of the following newspapers: *Boston Globe* (October 3–12, 1903), *New York Times* (October 2–12, 1905), *Chicago Tribune* (October 10–15, 1906).

Peter Morton Coan's *Ellis Island Interviews* assisted in painting a picture of the environment of the immigration station. Accounts of the fire that occurred in June 1897 can be found in the *New York Tribune* (June 15–16, 1897).

Descriptions of the Lower East Side were based upon *Jewish East Side*, edited by Milton Hindus; *The Promised City* by Moses Rischin; and *Lower East Side: A Guide to Its Jewish Past* by Ronald Sanders.

The 1893 Chicago World's Fair is described extensively in Eric Larson's *Devil in the White City*.

For the scenes occurring at St. Mary's Industrial School for Boys, I relied upon the writings of Brother Gilbert, collected and edited by Harry Rothgerber in his book *Young Babe Ruth*.

For an exciting account of America's fascination with Horatio Nelson's drive across the nation, read Dayton Duncan's *Horatio's Drive: America's First Road Trip*.

The devotional excerpts in chapter two come from Thomas à Kempis's *The Imitation of Christ*.

John McGraw and Christy Mathewson are perhaps the two men who had the greatest influence on the game during the first twenty years of the twentieth century. The books relied upon in building the narrative were Frank Deford's *The Old Ball Game*; Bob Gaines's *Christy Mathewson, the Christian Gentleman;* Ray Robinson's *Matty*; Christy Mathewson's *Pitching in a Pinch*; and John McGraw's *My Thirty Years in Baseball*.